THE
WITCH
RETURNS

THE
WITCH
RETURNS

Phyllis Reynolds Naylor

ILLUSTRATED BY

Joe Burleson

**Delacorte
Press**

Published by
Delacorte Press
Bantam Doubleday Dell Publishing Group, Inc.
666 Fifth Avenue
New York, New York 10103

Library of Congress Cataloging in Publication Data

Naylor, Phyllis Reynolds.
    The witch returns / Phyllis Reynolds Naylor : illustrated by Joe Burleson.
        p. cm.
    Summary: Convinced that the old woman who recently moved into the neighborhood is really the "dead" Mrs. Tuggle, Lynn and Mouse try to find help in withstanding her witchcraft.
    ISBN 0-385-30601-6
    [1. Witchcraft—Fiction.] I. Burleson, Joe, ill. II. Title.
PZ7.N24Wki   1992
[Fic]—dc20   91-32370
                                                        CIP
                                                        AC

Manufactured in the United States of America

September 1992

10 9 8 7 6 5 4 3 2 1

FFG

To Jaime Hinton and her sister, Corie

THE
WITCH
RETURNS

chapter one

Everyone knew now except Mother. Stevie, of course, was too young to understand, but Lynn had told her father and Judith everything.

Everything. It was a wonderful word—a wonderful feeling to know that nothing was held back. Better still to know that she and Marjorie Beasley (Mouse, as friends called her), didn't have to keep secrets anymore. In addition to her own family, Lynn had also told Dr. Long, a psychologist for the county schools, and Mouse had told *her* father. That meant six people knowing: three grown-ups, three girls.

What they knew about, of course, was the witchcraft—that it was there. *Had* been there, anyway. Now, perhaps, gone forever.

"What are you girls talking about so seriously out here?" Mother asked late one afternoon in September when Lynn, her sister Judith, and Mouse were whispering together on the back porch.

And Lynn put on her cheeriest face, answering, "Oh, everything, Mom. What do you want to know?"

"I want to know what's going on in your lives, what's happening at school. Things like that. No one ever tells me anything anymore." Mother sat down on the wicker chair across from them with an iced tea in her hand. "Maybe I intruded on some boy talk?" She smiled.

The girls giggled in protest, and Judith launched into the subject of how girls made better friends than boys. She would think so, of course, having just broken up with Ken Phillips.

But the fact was they hadn't been talking about boys at all, they had been talking about *It*. The *W* word: Witchcraft. Lynn hated when they lied to Mother. But the decision ultimately had been Dad's.

"Lynn," he had said once. "I'd really prefer that your mother not know any of this. Not yet, anyway."

They were all still worried about Mother, who had been under Mrs. Tuggle's influence longer than any of the others. *Had* she completely recovered from the old woman's spell? Or had Mrs. Tuggle's witchcraft never released her entirely? If given the chance, would Mother be drawn to some trace, some remnant, of the evil that kept recurring from time to time in the neighborhood?

The family didn't know, and was taking no chances. Lynn had even been keeping a journal for a year and a half, yet she wrote in secret. Someday she hoped to be able to hand it to Mother and say, "Maybe this will help you understand." She had recently tacked a note onto the very beginning, which said:

Dear Mom:
You don't know how often I've wished I could sit
down and tell you all this face-to-face. It's because I
love you that I can't. We all love you, and know that
after Mrs. Tuggle died in the fire, things were very hard
for you for a while. We didn't want to worry you more.
But I've kept a journal of what has happened to us ever
since we got mixed up with Mrs. Tuggle and her witch-
craft, and I've described as best I can what I saw—or
think I saw—and heard.
Lovingly, Lynn.

She began with her feeling that her older sister was
changing a year and a half ago, when Judith first
started going up the hill to sew at old Mrs. Tuggle's
house, and how strange Lynn had thought it was
when she found Judith down by Cowden's Creek,
crooning one of Elnora Tuggle's songs, while tad-
poles swam right into her cupped hands.

It was about that time that Lynn and Mouse had
discovered a rare book called *Spells and Potions* in
Mr. Beasley's secondhand bookstore, and the things
it said that witches do described some of the things
Judith and Mrs. Tuggle seemed to be doing. One day
a boy appeared, whom Mrs. Tuggle claimed to be
her grandson visiting from Michigan, but he looked
exactly like the photo in her living room of a boy she
said was her brother, who had come, when he was
young, from England with her and her husband
years ago. According to Mrs. Tuggle, he later
drowned in Cowden's Creek and was buried in the
cemetery.

What was most alarming to Lynn and Mouse was

a paragraph in *Spells and Potions* telling what a witch must do to attain her highest powers. One thing she might do was to give a baby brother or sister away to the witches, and when Lynn discovered Judith and this boy Clyde trying to take Stevie out on the porch one midnight, Lynn had screamed so hysterically that it upset their plan and Mrs. Tuggle, too, who had been caring for the Morley children that weekend while their parents were gone.

Judith and Clyde claimed they merely wanted to show Stevie a meteor shower, but according to the book, young witches and warlocks had only to put a small child on a porch at midnight and other witches would carry him off, since they used the fat of unbaptized infants and babies to grease their broomsticks. Stevie, having been christened but not baptized, seemed—in Lynn's eyes—a perfect offering.

It was right after that that Judith got sick, Clyde disappeared (went back to Michigan, Mrs. Tuggle said), and when Judith recovered, she seemed to have little memory of what had gone on with the old woman and no further interest in visiting her again. But that was only the beginning. . . .

Lynn couldn't think about the rest right now, because Mother was studying her from the wicker chair. Mrs. Morley's hair was pulled back away from her face, the way Lynn liked it, and tied with a scarf.

"Hmm?" Lynn heard her mother say, and realized she'd been asked a question. "Do *you* think girls make better friends than boys?"

"Well, *sure*! So far, anyway," Lynn said, and then she blushed when Mouse nudged her and laughed.

Mrs. Morley took a sip of iced tea. "I can't believe how my family has grown this past summer. Stevie in first grade now, Lynn in seventh, Judith in high school ... where does the time go? And Marjorie, you've grown a couple inches, it seems. Doesn't your father think so?"

"He *knows* so!" Mouse said. "We had to get practically all new clothes for me for junior high."

"Well, it can't be all bad then," Mother said.

Girl talk. Mouse loved to come to the Morleys', Lynn knew. Ever since her own mother had left the family a year ago, and would probably get a divorce, Marjorie seemed hungry for love. Not that Mr. Beasley wasn't a good father. He just couldn't be a mother too.

Lynn walked Mouse home before dinner. Most of the sidewalks were brick in this old Indiana town, and all the homes on Lynn's street were big and rambling, with bay windows, gables, and porches that ran all the way around. Marjorie lived on a side street farther down the steep hill, and if the girls weren't riding bikes, they always walked each other home. Sometimes they were talking so intently that when they got to one house they would turn around and start in the other direction, forgetting who was walking whom home.

"So what's your dad upset about?" Lynn asked. That was what they had been talking about on the porch with Judith before Mother came out and interrupted.

"The fire. Your setting the field on fire. He said

that people might begin to think that maybe it wasn't lightning that set Mrs. Tuggle's house on fire last spring; maybe you started that one, too."

"But I *didn't!*"

"*I* know you didn't, Lynn, and Dad knows you didn't. It's just that he's heard people talking about why there were two fires up here in a row."

"Well, I can't help what some people say. Dad always says 'Just tell the truth,' and that's what I've done." The corners of her mouth sagged. "Except with Mom," she added softly.

"But *my* dad says that if people talk about you, they're going to talk about me because we're together all the time."

Lynn stopped in her tracks and faced Marjorie. "Mouse, does he want us to stop being friends?"

Marjorie's eyes grew wide behind her big owl-like glasses. "No! He'd *never* say that. He just doesn't want us to get into any more trouble, that's all."

"Well, neither do I!" Lynn stopped when they reached the corner. "See you tomorrow?"

"After my piano lesson," Mouse said, and went on home.

Lynn turned and started back up the hill. Lights were coming on here and there as people began making dinner. Large gray clouds, rimmed in red, covered most of the sky, and the September air still blew warm and soft against her skin.

It was only six weeks ago that the night sky had blazed orange above the field behind Lynn's home. In a desperate attempt to get rid of the witch weed that was growing there, Lynn had set fire to those purple-hooded flowers, and could have burned down the neighborhood, she realized.

The firemen, of course, had taken statements from Lynn and her father, but she had been very careful not to say anything about witchcraft. She had simply said that the weeds were taking over the field, that their scent was making the family ill, and she had tried using weed killer on them, which hadn't worked. So, she said, she had circled the weeds with gasoline, set them afire, and no, she would never do such a thing again and was sorry she had caused so much trouble.

Lynn had to go to the fire station, accompanied by her father, for a lecture on public safety and a lesson in fire prevention. The five girls from school who had been lured to the field by the witch weed, Lynn was sure, and had started a witch's coven, with Mouse a member-to-be, had become mysteriously ill after the fire, and—just as had happened to Judith after she recovered—lost whatever powers they'd had before. Lynn was *glad* she had burned the witch weed. Glad, glad, glad! She'd do anything to save Mouse. To stop the witchcraft. If she *had*.

The Morleys had taken their vacation at the Indiana Dunes the last week of August, as they'd planned, and when Lynn and Mouse began junior high school the first week of September, the girls from school who had started the coven were now as friendly as they'd been back in sixth grade.

But by now even Dr. Long believed that something strange was going on in the neighborhood. Like Lynn's father, he was reluctant to call it

witchcraft—didn't want to give it any label at all—
but agreed that things had happened he simply
couldn't explain.

"Then let's let it rest there," Mouse's father had
said at the conference Dr. Long had called. "Let's
help our girls put this Mrs. Tuggle business behind
them, and get involved in something else."

And everyone at the conference agreed—all but
Lynn's mother, who wasn't there. It was also agreed
that there would be nothing kept secret—except
from Mother, of course. Anything suspicious noticed by one should be shared with them all. And if
things seemed again to be getting out of control, the
grown-ups this time—Dr. Long, Mr. Morley, and
Mr. Beasley—would decide what to do. *Not* the
girls. It was fine with Lynn and Mouse. Fine with
Judith too. If Lynn never heard the words *Tuggle,*
witch, or *witchcraft* again, she wouldn't care a bit.

She had reached her house now and dusk was just
settling over the street. It used to be so peaceful here
on the hill—the big quiet houses with their gingerbread trim. She was about to turn in at the sidewalk when something gleamed through the trees
farther on. She wasn't sure why she stopped. It
could be anything at all, but the more she thought,
the more disturbed she felt. The moon was coming
up behind her, not up there at the top of the hill, so it
couldn't be the moon.

There were no streetlights back there either, not
where that gleam was coming from. Nor did it
flicker on and off, so it couldn't be a firefly.

Drawn to the gleam, Lynn passed her own house and went on. Past the house next to hers, the house next to that, then on past the large stretch of empty lot to the thick trees beyond. Behind the trees, she knew, in the clearing at the very top of the hill, a new house had been built over the ashes of Mrs. Tuggle's old one—a house that resembled in every way the house of Elnora Tuggle.

Lynn stared through the branches of the thorn apple tree that hid the door of the house from view. There was a light on in an upper window; that was the gleam. Yet as far as Lynn knew, the owners had not yet moved in. The window was where the old sewing room had been, where Judith had spent so many hours with Mrs. Tuggle—learning to cut a pattern and sew a seam, the old woman had told Lynn—but Lynn had every reason to believe it was witchcraft as well that Judith had been learning about.

She stepped boldly out from behind the thorn apple tree, right onto the narrow sidewalk that led up to the house, and stared straight up at the window. If she was going to report facts, she wanted to get them straight this time. She would not say she had seen something she only thought she had seen. She'd stand there until she saw something—someone—definite. Then she could go home and tell her father.

But as soon as she planted herself on the front sidewalk and looked straight up, the light went out, and only the dark shape of the house remained, silhouetted against the sky.

chapter two

"There was a light on in Mrs. Tuggle's house," Lynn said as she walked into the living room, where her father and Judith were finishing a puzzle they had started at home the last day of vacation.

"It's not Mrs. Tuggle's house anymore," Judith reminded her. "We don't know who owns the new one."

"Well, anyway, there was a light in an upstairs window, and the moving van hasn't even come yet."

"Sometimes people arrive early to fix their house up; don't worry about it, Lynn," said her father, finding a corner piece to the puzzle and putting it in.

"I'm not," Lynn told him. "But you said to tell you if anything unusual ever happened again, so I'm telling you that there was a light on, that's all." Lynn sprawled on the couch and picked up a *National Geographic* from the coffee table.

For a few minutes there was quiet in the room, broken only by an occasional "Hmmm" from her father, or the quiet tapping of a puzzle piece against the card table as Judith looked for a place to put it. Lynn could hear Stevie's chatter out in the kitchen as Mother made dinner. And then, almost as an afterthought, Mr. Morley said, "By the way, girls, I think it would be better if you didn't go up there."

"Up where?" Judith asked absently, still studying the puzzle.

"Up to the new house—where Mrs. Tuggle used to live. Just stay away from there. Okay?"

"Why?" Lynn asked.

"I think it would be best," Father answered, which as far as Lynn was concerned was no explanation at all. She was about to ask more when six-year-old Stevie came skipping into the room.

"Guess what we're having for dinner?" he said, diving onto the couch next to Lynn.

"Frogs' eyes."

"No!"

"Asparagus pudding."

"Yuk! No!" Stevie giggled.

"Cream of pigeon soup?"

Stevie howled. "No, silly! Chicken and corn on the cob and biscuits."

"Sounds good to me," said Father.

"Look! I found another corner piece!" said Judith as Mother called them to dinner.

Stevie went racing back to the kitchen again, Judith behind him, but just as Mr. Morley got up from the card table Lynn asked, "Why, Dad?"

"I *told* you why. Because I think it's best."

"That wouldn't be the kind of answer you'd take from me."

"No, because you're the kid and I'm the dad around here. Okay? Sometimes what I think is best is the only reason you're going to get. Got it?" He was not smiling, she noticed.

Lynn just shrugged and followed him to the kitchen. No, she didn't "get it" at all. She knew perfectly well that her dad was holding something back, but she also knew she wasn't going to get anywhere badgering him.

It was a good dinner, and everyone seemed hungry except Father. He didn't eat his usual three pieces of chicken, only one. Only one biscuit, too, and though he smiled at the others and nodded occasionally, it seemed to Lynn that his thoughts were somewhere else.

For a moment a thought almost too awful occurred to Lynn. This was the way that Mother had begun to act when the witchcraft first got a hold on her. The silences, the far-off look in the eyes. Lynn studied her father as he thoughtfully buttered his biscuit. *No!* She could not stand it if Father, the one person in the family who had not seemed affected so far, were to be caught up in the spell. Not *two* parents! But she also knew that men as well as women were strong in some ways and weak in others. She didn't know in what ways her father might be weak. Perhaps he had simply not been tested yet.

Lynn was the one who resembled her father, with a long face that looked as though it had been stretched just a bit and pale skin lightly sprinkled with freckles. Judith and Stevie looked like Mother, with their round faces and wide-set eyes. And tonight Mrs. Morley seemed more like a real mother again—glad to have served a meal everyone liked, eager to hear about everyone's day. Not that she didn't have a life of her own apart from the family, because Mother wrote children's books, and there was a whole shelf of them in the living room, with bright-colored jackets, and the name *Sylvia Jackson Morley* on every one.

"Homework tonight?" Mother asked, serving dessert.

"On Friday night?" Judith said. "I *never* do homework on Friday night."

"I do," said Lynn, "just so I can have Saturday and Sunday to do what I want."

Everyone helped with the dishes, and then Judith went back to the jigsaw puzzle, and Lynn went upstairs to the third-floor bedroom she shared with Judith. She found the place in her journal where she had told about Judith trying to take Stevie out on the porch at midnight, and read on from there; she wanted to read it with her mother's eyes, as Mother would read it someday.

What had happened next, after Clyde went back to Michigan and Judith stopped going to Mrs. Tuggle's, was that a huge and hideous cat moved into the old woman's house—a stray, she had said. The terrifying thing about it was that it wore, around its neck, a spider medallion, the same kind of charm that the boy—Mrs. Tuggle's brother—in the old photo was wearing.

What had bothered Lynn in particular was that Mrs. Tuggle seemed to have her eye on Mouse next—poor vulnerable Mouse, so unhappy because her parents had just separated. The old woman found excuses to invite Mouse into her home, and always gave her tea, made from creek water, that seemed to put Marjorie into a trance. And then nine crows began following Mouse wherever she went, distracting her at school, affecting her homework, making her terrified. And down at the creek one day, the girls saw Mrs. Tuggle standing with her arms outstretched, chanting. There on her arms perched the nine black crows.

Lynn had gathered up her courage and gone to Mrs. Tuggle's, accusing her of witchcraft and threatening to tell the whole town if she didn't leave Mouse alone. And the old woman had smiled as Lynn went out the door, her gold tooth gleaming, and said, "I'm a lot older than you, Lynn girl, and much, much wiser. Take care that you don't turn the spirits against you." And Lynn had heard her laughing even after the door closed.

"Whew!" Lynn put the journal down and hugged herself. Would she never be able to think about what had happened without this terror inching up her back? Instinctively she glanced all around the room, looking for shadows, listening for whispers. And finally, when she was convinced that she was safe here in her bedroom, she took a deep breath and picked up the journal once more.

It was not only Mouse the woman had seemed to be after next, but Stevie, who was lured by the cat. Why, after all those years of living in the neighborhood peacefully—or so Lynn thought—was the old woman trying to form a coven of witches now? And the answer came in something Lynn had overheard her father, a lawyer for the county, say to her mother: No death certificate seemed to have been filed for Mrs. Tuggle's brother years ago when, according to the old woman, he had drowned. The county was preparing to move all the graves in the old cemetery to a newer one across town, and were contacting the family members of the deceased.

If, as Lynn suspected, Mrs. Tuggle's brother was *not* in his coffin, the old woman might have good reason not to want his grave touched. And if she had seven people to make up a coven of witches, she might have just enough power to prevent this from happening.

What both Lynn and Mouse had suspected was that Mrs. Tuggle's brother had not drowned at all— that the woman had bodily transformed him into something else, which, according to *Spells and Potions*, witches can do—and brought him back from time to time as this or that, depending on when she needed him most. She would need him the most when she had six people to form her coven and needed a seventh. If she brought him back as her "familiar," a witch's servant, he could well have been the cat. Needing to explain his absence long ago in the neighborhood, however, she had simply claimed he had drowned, and that she and her husband had buried him themselves.

But then, when Marjorie brought *Spells and Potions* home from the bookstore to see if there were any charms they could use to protect them from whatever Mrs. Tuggle might try next, her huge cat had got into the Beasleys' house and torn the rare book to shreds. Eventually, of course, Mr. Beasley had been able to get another copy of the book for his store, but when Lynn tried to tell her parents what was happening—how worried she was about Mouse—her parents had quarreled as to whose fault it was that Lynn's imagination got her into so much trouble. Lynn vowed she would not bring up the subject again.

What came next in her journal was so awful that Lynn had to get up and get a drink of water before she read it. Had to walk about her bedroom to reassure herself that she was here and this was now. She went down to the bathroom on the second floor, filled a cup with water, and stood in the hallway a moment, listening to the comforting sounds of her family below.

"Mom," she called, "do you want me to read Stevie his story tonight?"

"*Would* you, Lynn? I've hardly had a minute to myself today, and that would be wonderful. He's just having a bedtime snack. In about ten minutes, maybe."

Lynn went back to her journal. What came next was the night Lynn had stayed over with Mouse because Mr. Beasley was out of town, and hundreds of cats and crows gathered outside, scratching and clawing to get in. The lead crow, scrambling down the chimney, had been killed as the girls closed the flue on him. That still, however, left the cat.

Lynn gathered up all Stevie's bath toys—his water wheel and rubber duck, his cups and boats—and sat on the lid of the toilet while her little brother had a naval battle. He finally gave in to a soft towel, warm pajamas, and his favorite book, *Little Bear's Visit*.

"Daddy's a *grump!*" Stevie said as Lynn closed the book after the last story. "I asked him to read it to me and he said no."

"Maybe he had things to do," Lynn said.

"He wasn't doing anything. He was staring out the window."

"Well, that's doing something." Lynn said, trying to make a joke of it. But her worries about Father returned.

With Stevie in bed, she went back to the third floor, determined to finish reading her journal that night and see if she had left out anything Mother should know. She was now up to last winter, when Mrs. Morley had rented an upstairs room in Mrs. Tuggle's house to use as a writing studio, and from then on, little by little, seemed to be withdrawing from the family. And the cat—the huge, hideous, demon cat—was always there, watching.

Lynn and Mouse had developed a plan. It was farfetched, and they'd known it, but Mouse had been studying a book on hypnotism, and they decided to catch the demon cat in a raccoon trap and hypnotize it. If, as they suspected, the cat was indeed Mrs. Tuggle's younger brother, bodily transformed, just waiting for her to transform him back again into a warlock to join her coven, then it might be possible that they could induce him—the cat— to talk.

They had lured him with cream and got him in

the trap, and Mouse took him home with the promise to call Lynn to come over after her father had gone to work. Lynn met Mrs. Tuggle out in the meadow, searching for her cat, and told her the animal was being held hostage; that they would only guarantee his safe return if, in turn, nothing happened to Lynn's mother while she was writing in Mrs. Tuggle's house.

But when Lynn got home, she had received a tearful phone call from Marjorie: The cat was dead. The girls suspected more than ever that Mrs. Tuggle, through witchcraft, had killed the cat herself so it could reveal no secrets, after first changing the cat, her brother, into something else—something that could leave the cage undetected: a snake, a mouse, a spider, even, and only the dead body of a cat would be left behind. The girls buried it out in the meadow, but Lynn first removed the spider medallion and slipped it in her pocket. Later, Stevie, at Mrs. Tuggle's request, found it and innocently gave it back to the old woman.

Then, finally, there was an unexpected stroke of good luck. In some books Mr. Beasley had bought at auction, Mouse found several pages from a diary of a woman named Bertha Voight, in which she had written that she suspected Elnora Tuggle of being a witch. The girls went to see Bertha Voight's brother, an elderly man, who confirmed that the two women had never got along, and that Bertha had even got hold of a trinket of some kind to protect her from Elnora Tuggle. Then, he sadly told the girls, the year Mrs. Tuggle's brother drowned—the year of the big flood—Bertha Voight herself disappeared, and her body was never found. It was assumed she had been washed away in the floodwaters. Now Lynn and Mouse were convinced that Mrs. Tuggle had caused her death.

Because Mother had seemed to be getting worse, more trancelike and drawn to Mrs. Tuggle, Judith had agreed to be hypnotized by Mouse to see what she could remember of things that had gone on when *she* was at Mrs. Tuggle's. And when she was under Marjorie's spell, she said that there was a treasure in a box on top of Mrs. Tuggle's cupboard in the sewing room, but she didn't know what— something important that had once belonged to someone else.

Lynn and Mouse had gone to Mrs. Tuggle's one night when the old woman was out, sneaked into the sewing room, and looked in the box on the cupboard. In it was a piece of chalk, and Mouse remembered reading in *Spells and Potions* that if you were to draw a circle around yourself with a piece of consecrated chalk, evil could not break through the circle to get to you. The chalk must have once belonged to Bertha Voight.

Lynn knew she could not read the next part up here in the bedroom by herself. It was far too frightening. So she took her journal to the floor below, ran water in the bathtub, and climbed in. Here she was protected by tiled walls and concrete. There were no shadows here as there were in the huge room above, and she could hear better the voices of the others downstairs.

"Is that you in there, Lynn?" Mother called as she passed.

"Yes, I'm just taking a soak."

"Okay. Take your time but let me know when you're through. I'm next," Mother told her.

Lynn took her washcloth, ran it under the hot water, then draped it over her chest, like a shield. Thus protected, she read the part that still sometimes came back to her in dreams, when she would wake up in a cold sweat—the part about Mrs. Tuggle coming back early, and the girls hiding in her cellar. Yet somehow the old woman had known they were there. When she came down to get them, Mouse hurriedly drew a circle around her and Lynn, to Mrs. Tuggle's fury, but the old woman called each of them by a name they had never heard before— "Dorolla" for Lynn, and "Sevena" for Mouse—and on hearing these names, they had almost been drawn from the circle. It was only because Mr. Morley had come looking for them, ringing the doorbell upstairs, that the spell had been broken and the girls escaped.

Finally, there had been another storm in town, another flood. Mrs. Morley, who had promised her husband she would not write any longer in Mrs. Tuggle's house, had gone up the hill to get her manuscript. Lynn, at home, felt increasingly worried for her. A call from her father, who was out inspecting the storm damage, said that in the flood of the night before, some of the coffins had been washed up out of their graves, that the coffin of Mrs. Tuggle's brother had sprung open, and the skeleton inside was not that of a young boy at all, but of a woman. *Bertha Voight.*

Lynn had rushed up the hill to get her mother, and lightning struck Mrs. Tuggle's house, setting it aflame. Lynn had climbed to the upstairs porch and rescued Mother just in time, because the house burst into flames and burned to the ground, Mrs. Tuggle in it. All that was left in the rubble was her green glass eye.

Lynn got out of the tub. There were two more pages to go, but she had been in long enough, and Mother would begin to wonder.

"You can have the tub now," she called as she wrapped her robe around her and padded back up-stairs. Why was she doing this to herself, she won-dered. If she read the rest, the terrible rest, she would have nightmares before morning. Why relive it all and make herself upset again?

She knew the answer before she asked. Always before, when she thought the witchcraft was over, or that Mrs. Tuggle had given up, Lynn would get a premonition when something was about to happen. An uneasiness, a fear, a deep sense of foreboding. And sure enough, in a matter of days something new and terrible would happen. And though she fought against it, struggled against it, she felt the same way now. *Was* it her father who was next on the list?

She wrapped her quilt around her, curled up in a corner of her bed, and leaned against the wall.

chapter three

"Finished!" Judith came upstairs with a bag of Fritos. "A thousand-piece jigsaw puzzle finished in four days!"

"Who did the most—you or Dad?" Lynn asked, putting her journal away.

"I did. Dad wasn't much help this time." Judith looked at Lynn curiously. "You cold?"

"A little."

"I don't think it's cold at all!" Judith held out the bag of Fritos and came over, plopping down on Lynn's bed.

Lynn took a handful, and somehow, with Judith in the room, she felt better. She herself never had the patience much for puzzles and games, and could not understand how her sister could keep at it for four nights. "Judith," she said, wondering, "Do you miss Kenny?"

"Ugh, ugh, and ugh," Judith said in reply.

"Well, it's something I don't understand," Lynn told her. "How can you be madly and deliriously in love with a boy one week and break up with him the next?"

"Because I found out he wasn't madly and deliriously in love with me," Judith said. "Any guy who

would give you his ID bracelet and take you to
movies and for walks in the moonlight, and then
invite another girl to go roller-skating with him,
can't be madly and deliriously in love with anyone
but himself. There are at least two—maybe three—
other girls in town who think Kenny Phillips is in
love with them, and I decided I wasn't going to be
one of them."

"So what are you going to do, Judith?" Lynn had
no idea what girls did after boys broke up with
them. Songs on the radio made it sound as though
you died of a broken heart or something.

Judith did not look as though she were about to
die. "Forget Kenny Phillips, number one. Help you
solve the Mystery of Mrs. Tuggle, number two."

Lynn looked at her curiously. "You figure there's
anything left to solve?"

There was a long pause. "What do you think,
Lynn?"

"Well, nothing's really been explained."

"Exactly."

Judith stretched out on Lynn's bed, her head at
the foot, feet up by Lynn. Lynn noticed that Judith
had painted her toenails pearl-pink. Lynn never
even painted her fingernails, much less her toenails.

"Do you ever wonder," Judith said, "what would
have happened if Stevie hadn't found Mrs. Tuggle's
glass eye in the ashes and thought it was a marble?
If he had left it there, instead of putting it in his
pocket, and the builders had bulldozed right over
it? Maybe the evil would have been trapped there
forever and nothing more would have happened."

"I wonder about that all the time," Lynn said. "I wonder if all these things would still have happened if Mouse and I hadn't thrown the eye into the creek. Would the witch weed have grown on the creek bank at all? Would it have attracted those girls from school to start a coven down in the meadow? Would Mouse have wanted to join? I *had* to do it, Judith. I *had* to set fire to the witch weed and see if I could stop it."

"I'm not blaming you. I could have done it myself."

"Those girls promised Mouse so much. To give her the power to bring her mother back from Ohio, for one thing. Mouse would do almost anything to get her mother back."

"I know. What are the girls like now at school?"

"Nice. Just like they were before. The fifth-grade twins are in sixth, of course, but Betty, Charlotte Ann, and Kirsten are in some of my classes at junior high, and they're all friendly, like they used to be, before the witch weed grew. They don't even talk about it. It's as though they don't remember."

"Just like me . . . like I was after I stopped going to Mrs. Tuggle's," Judith mused.

"The thing that worries me the most are the names Mrs. Tuggle gave to Mouse and me: Sevena and Dorolla. When she called us by those names, it felt as though we had to do whatever she told us, as though she was calling on some evil inside of *us*. That's what I don't like to think about, Judith. That there's something inside of me I can't control."

"Everyone is capable of being bad, Lynn. What's

dangerous is thinking you can't control it, because you can. We talked about that in Social Studies last year—about telling yourself that something or someone *made* you do things. Nobody *makes* you do them; you do them yourself."

Judith went back on her side of the room, which was divided in half by a curtain, then turned on her radio. For the next half hour she tried on fall clothes, holding them up against her at the mirror and dropping in a pile those that she didn't want anymore so Lynn could try them on. Lynn finished reading her journal—the part about the eye— adding a note here and there to make it clearer, should Mother ever read it. At last Judith called good night and turned out her lamp, and Lynn turned out hers a short time later.

Suddenly, Judith's voice came softly from the other side of the curtain: "Lynn, come look!"

"What is it?" Lynn got out of bed in the darkness and went over to Judith's side. She could see Judith silhouetted against the window, crouching down with her arms on the sill.

"What is it?" Lynn said again, kneeling down beside her. And then she saw.

There in the backyard was a large gray rabbit— perhaps the largest rabbit Lynn had ever seen. It hopped a few paces, then stopped, holding perfectly still. Hopped a few more paces, stopped. In the paleness of moonlight it was the only visible thing in the yard.

"Is it wild, do you suppose?" Lynn asked.

"I imagine. I don't know how anyone could let a pet rabbit loose and expect it to come back."

They watched a while longer.

"It's so huge. It *must* belong to somebody," Lynn said finally. "I don't think wild rabbits would be so fat."

Judith yawned at last, and crawled into bed, but Lynn continued to watch from the window. She didn't know why, but she didn't think the rabbit was wild, didn't think the rabbit was tame, and wasn't at all sure that the rabbit might not, in fact, be something, or someone, else entirely.

A moving truck came grinding up the hill on Saturday.

"Well! Neighbors at last!" Mother said.

Lynn's father said nothing. Absolutely nothing. Stood at the bay window in the music room overlooking the street, watching the driver of the van leaning forward, checking the addresses. Then he went into the dining room to work on his papers. Father's papers always took up half the table, and when he was working on his briefs, as lawyers called them, the Morley children knew better than to interrupt.

Mouse came over as she'd promised after she took her piano lesson, and the first thing she said when Lynn met her on the porch was "Somebody's moving in."

"I know. We saw the van go by."

"You want to go up and watch?"

Lynn knew exactly what her father had said about going up there, but she reasoned it this way: By "up there" he meant the house on the hill. He did not say, in so many words, that she could never ride her bike to the top of the hill and down again, as she'd been doing since she was seven years old. And if she was going to ride to the top of the hill, there was no reason at all she could not stop for a few minutes to catch her breath, once she got there, just to see what sort of stuff they were moving in.

"Okay," she said, and got her bike from the side of the house. "How was your music lesson?"

"Lousy. I've been on Bach's Air for the G String for a month and a half, and I've still not got it. I could be on it for six months more and wouldn't have it. I'm hopeless."

"Do you like piano?"

"No."

"Then why are you taking lessons?"

"Because Mom likes to hear me play."

Lynn had the sense not to say *But your mom doesn't live with you anymore.* She said, "Well, maybe by the time you visit her again, you'll play it beautifully."

"Maybe," said Mouse.

They got to the top of the hill and parked their bikes across the street from the house that had been built over Mrs. Tuggle's ashes.

"So who's moving in?" Mouse asked.

"I don't know. I saw a light in a window last night, though."

"You did?"

Lynn nodded. "But when I walked up there and stared at it from the sidewalk, it went out."

Mouse glanced at her quickly, over the rims of her huge glasses. "Did you tell your dad?"

"Yes."

"What did he say?"

"Not to come up here anymore."

"But . . . !" Mouse looked around uneasily.

"I know. He meant the *house*. He couldn't have meant that I can't ride to the top of the hill ever again. *Besides*, Mouse, he's not being entirely truthful himself."

"How do you mean?"

"I mean that he wouldn't tell me *why* he said that. And I don't think he'd have said it if he didn't know something that we don't, and the agreement was that there wouldn't be any secrets anymore." What she didn't add was that perhaps Father didn't even know why himself.

"Look." Mouse interrupted her.

The Mayflower movers were placing a ramp at the side of the van and rolling out huge dark pieces of furniture. The first to come was a tall bureau with eight drawers, and feet on the bottom that looked like lion's claws. After that, a large oval table, made of mahogany, with the same clawlike feet.

"It looks just like some of Mrs. Tuggle's old stuff," said Mouse.

Lynn was thinking the same thing. She thought if she watched long enough, she would see the husband or wife of the family come to the door and talk to the movers; see a child or teenager at one of the windows. But no one appeared at the door. No one looked out a window.

"Let's go," Mouse said at last, so they raced down the hill, into the center of town—past the bank, past the library, Mr. Beasley's bookstore, and went to the Sweet Shoppe for ice cream while the weather was still warm.

Betty, Charlotte Ann, and Kirsten were there in a booth, and immediately scooted over to make room for Lynn and Mouse.

"They have a new flavor," Charlotte Ann said. "Mocha cherry. It's good! Try a bite of mine." Lynn did, and it was.

After Mouse had ordered a cone for each of them, Kirsten said, "I'm having a birthday party next Saturday at two. Can you come? We might go skating or something."

"Sure!" Lynn said. "Give us some hints of what you want for your birthday. Clothes?"

"Urk," said Kirsten.

"Tapes?"

"Umm . . . maybe."

"Something to eat?"

"If it's as good as this ice cream."

After the other three girls had left, and Lynn and Mouse had the booth to themselves, Mouse said, "I got a letter from Mom this morning."

"What'd she say?"

"The usual. She loves me. She misses me. But she knows I'm happier being with Dad than I would be with her. The thing is . . ." Mouse licked at the bottom of her cone where the ice cream was beginning to drip. "The thing is, she never *asks* me where I'd rather live. She tells me. It's as though she's afraid of my answer. As though I just might say that no, I want to come and live with her in Ohio. So she doesn't give me that chance."

Lynn never knew what to say when Mouse talked about her mother. She certainly didn't want to say anything that would make Marjorie feel worse. But neither did she want to give her false hope. So she said, "Some mothers just leave and never even write their kids, Mouse. Your mother not only writes, but tells you she loves you. I'm sure she really does."

"I hope so," said Mouse.

That's the way the conversations always went. Hoping.

Mouse hung around that evening long enough to be invited to dinner, since her father was working late, and Lynn's mother was glad to have her. They were having ravioli, one of Marjorie's favorites, and Mouse volunteered to do the dishes afterward, so of course Lynn said she'd help, while Mother and Judith played duets on the piano.

It was out in the backyard later—beyond the garden, actually—that Lynn saw the rabbit again. She and Mouse had opened the gate and gone down to the creek to see if the grass was starting to grow again after the fire (it was), and whether the purple-hooded flowers were really, truly gone (they were), when they saw the large gray rabbit coming across the footbridge. It took a few steps and stopped, nose wriggling, just as it had before.

"It's huge, Lynn!" said Mouse. "Lordy! A mutant rabbit!"

"Judith and I saw it from our window last night."

"Is it tame?"

"I don't think so."

The girls stood without moving until the rabbit had crossed the bridge, not wanting it to feel trapped. Then, when it was closer, they moved slowly forward. Whenever it stopped eating, they stopped moving. When it began to eat again, they edged forward a little.

It must *be tame*, Lynn thought as they got nearer and nearer the rabbit, and still it didn't run. And then suddenly, as though seeing them for the first time, its huge dark eye rolled in their direction, and a strange high pitched sound came from its throat.

The girls stared. Lynn never knew that rabbits made any noise at all, certainly not a sound like that. And then it was gone, leaping gracefully over the new weeds and clover, until it had disappeared in the dusk.

"So much for a pet rabbit," Mouse said. "I would have liked one, though. I'd have taken really good care of it."

On Monday after school, after Mouse had stopped by the Morleys' for a snack, then gone to her father's bookstore, and Judith had taken Stevie to his swimming lesson at the Y, Mother said, "These cinnamon rolls are just about done, Lynn, and there's some chicken salad in the refrigerator. Want to go with me to take them to our new neighbors?"

Lynn stared. Her first thought was to say *Dad doesn't want us up there*, but she knew she could not. Mother would ask too many questions and Lynn would have to tell her too much. Nor could she stay home and allow Mother to go alone. Her father would *especially* not want that.

"Uhh . . ." She stalled. "Who are they? Have you met them?"

"No, and no one else has either. *Somebody* around here has to be friendly. The moving van was here on Saturday, and I've seen a light on through the trees once or twice, so *some*body's got to be there. We can at least go see."

"Maybe you should wait until Dad comes home and *both* of you go," Lynn suggested.

"Good heavens, no. He won't be home until seven tonight, and by then the new folks would have had their dinner. I want to take the rolls up while they're still hot."

"Okay." There was absolutely nothing else Lynn could do.

She waited while her mother took the pan from the oven, let the rolls cool a few minutes, then deftly slipped them onto a plate.

"You carry the rolls, I'll carry the chicken salad, and if the new people aren't home, we'll eat it ourselves," Mother said. "Actually, I put some aside for our own supper anyway."

The air had turned cooler on Sunday and now it

was cold enough for sweaters. Already someone had
started a fire in a fireplace, because the air had a
sharp smoky smell that Lynn always loved in the
fall.

"Almost pumpkin time!" Mother said gaily, turning her face up to get the last rays of afternoon sun.

They passed the two houses next to theirs, then
the long stretch of emptiness and the clump of
spruce trees. Finally the new house came into view,
dark against the sky. Clouds gathered overhead that
showed purple around the edges, and the chimney
of the house seemed to reach out from the roof and
touch it, like the spire on a church. The thorn apple
tree in the front yard, the tree untouched by the fire,
stood guard, blocking the front door completely
from view.

Mother stopped for a moment and took a good
look. "That's Mrs. Tuggle's design exactly. Someone
must have had those plans and simply re-created
her old house. In a way, it's nice to have it back,
don't you think?"

Lynn said nothing because she did not want to lie.
No it was *not* nice, and she did *not* want a replica of
the old house to remind her of Mrs. Tuggle. She
hoped the people living in it now were young with
lots of small children, something to make new
memories out of a place that had been so horrible
before. Had Mother already forgotten the terror of
her last day there?

Lynn pushed aside the branches of the thorn apple and led the way up the narrow sidewalk to the

door, as though making a barrier of her body between the house and her mother. There were no
lights on inside.

Her skin felt cold when she saw the brass door-
knocker, the same hideous thing that Mrs. Tuggle
had had on hers. It looked like a troll with its tongue
hanging out. She remembered how, always before,
when she had knocked on Mrs. Tuggle's door, the
eyes of the troll seemed to be moving, until she
discovered that the troll had no eyes at all, only
holes where the eyes should be, so that whoever was
inside the house could look out and see who the
visitors were. She stared intently at the new door
knocker. There were holes where the eyes should be.
Goose bumps rose up on her arms. Lynn swallowed,
and banged the knocker.

She wanted in the worst way to go home. If she
had been there with Mouse, they would have set the
food on the doorstep, banged the knocker, and run
before anyone could answer.

From somewhere deep inside, she heard muffled
footsteps, soft footsteps, slow footsteps, until the
creak of a board told her that someone was standing
just behind the door. A pause. An uncomfortable
pause when Lynn was sure that the eyes of the troll
moved.

And then the door opened, and from out of the
shadows emerged an old woman, small, and somewhat bent, with shoulders that stuck up through her
dress like doorknobs, and strong, gnarled hands
that clutched a spoon.

Lynn could hear her mother's quick intake of

air—an almost imperceptible gasp that showed either surprise or fear, Lynn wasn't sure.

The old woman tipped her bony face up toward them and said, "Ah! Visitors, is it? Come to see the new neighbor? Well, come in, my lovelies, come in!"

chapter four

Lynn knew instinctively that they should not go inside. They should thrust the rolls and chicken salad into the old woman's hands, say "Welcome to the neighborhood," and leave.

She also knew that there was no way she could persuade her mother to do that. Mrs. Morley had always been a friendly, gracious person, and it wasn't in her nature to be so abrupt. Yet Lynn noticed that even she hesitated when she came face-to-face with their new neighbor.

"We . . . we thought you might like some supper, just having moved in and all," Mother said, holding the bowl out in front of her. "I'm Sylvia Morley, and this is Lynn."

Without taking the dishes offered, the elderly woman edged farther back into the shadows, holding the door wide open, forcing Lynn and her mother to carry the food in themselves.

Like a spider in her web, Lynn thought.

Mother stepped into the hallway and paused again, reluctant, it seemed, to go on. "Well, it certainly looks as though you've settled right in," she said, glancing about. "Shades on your lamps already, pictures on your walls. We do hope you like it here, Miss . . . uh . . ."

"Gullone. Mrs. Gullone," the woman said. "Ah! There hasn't been the smell of homemade cinnamon rolls in this house until now. Will you put them on my table, then?" And she led the way to the kitchen.

In some ways Mrs. Gullone's house was just like the Morleys', the same entrance hall, same storage closet under the stairs, same music room off to the right. . . . But in other ways the house was different—the porch on the second story, for example, that enveloped the front of the house. In every way, however, the house was the same as Mrs. Tuggle's, and the more Lynn studied the old woman, as much of her as she could see in the half-darkness, the more Mrs. Gullone seemed to resemble Elnora Tuggle.

"We'll have us a sit-down in the parlor," said Mrs. Gullone, "and you shall tell me all about yourselves."

Will you come into my parlor? said the spider to the fly. . . .

"I've just come from England, you see, and have much to learn about my new neighborhood," the woman continued.

It was beginning all over again, Lynn was sure, and it was all she could do to keep from saying *Don't play games with us, Mrs. Tuggle; we know it's you.*

"Now," the woman said, when the food had been deposited on the kitchen table. "I shall make some

tea to go with the cinnamon rolls." She turned on
the kitchen light.

"Oh, no, the food is all for you," Mother said
quickly. "Please enjoy it."

"And we don't drink tea," Lynn added emphatically, knowing the effect Mrs. Tuggle's tea had had
on Mother before. Mrs. Morley raised her eyebrows
at such rudeness, but Lynn continued: "We just
stopped by to say hello."

She saw that Mrs. Gullone was studying her intently, and gathered up the courage to stare back.
And then her breath stopped, her lungs seemed to
freeze, for as she gazed into the old woman's face,
with its strong chin and heavy brows, she saw that
one of Mrs. Gullone's eyes was gray, the other green.
And before she could stop herself, she said, "I think I
know who you are."

Mother jerked about and stared at Lynn, but Mrs.
Gullone simply smiled, and as her lips stretched
wider and wider a gold tooth gleamed from the back
of her mouth.

Then the smile disappeared. "So I look like my
sister, do I? Ah, but that I could bring her back.
People sometimes thought we were twins, but in
truth Elnora was a year older. The most I could do, I
thought, was to rebuild the house she had loved. So
here I am, fresh from Castletown, to live out my life
as Elnora would have done. Come. Sit down." She
brushed past them with the cinnamon rolls and
some plates and led the way to the parlor.

Lynn glanced at her mother, but Mrs. Morley

followed the old woman and sat down on the worn velvet sofa. Lynn felt confused. If this was Elnora Tuggle's sister, then it did make sense that she should inherit the property and that she might want to rebuild her sister's house. But when Lynn sat down beside her mother and looked around, everything was arranged just as it had been before—the same kinds of dark heavy furniture in exactly the same places; the yellowed lace curtains, the same little saucers and photographs, almost identical to the ones that had burned to ashes. A great uneasiness swept over her.

To insure that a witch's power dies with her, *Spells and Potions* had said, her ashes must be scattered to the four winds. Mrs. Tuggle's ashes had definitely not been scattered—simply bulldozed under. But not before Stevie had found her green glass eye.

Lynn sat silently by as her mother and Mrs. Gullone compared the weather on the Isle of Man in England and the weather in Indiana. What if Mrs. Tuggle had *not* died in the fire, as everyone thought she had? What if, somehow, miraculously, she had escaped and gone into hiding, leaving her eye behind? What if, at the last moment, amid smoke and flames, she had bodily transfigured herself into something else, which had gone unnoticed, and now she was back, masquerading as her own sister. Because Elnora Tuggle had been officially declared dead, no charges, obviously, could be brought against her for the suspected murder of her longtime enemy, Bertha Voight.

"Hmmm?"

She startled when she realized that the old woman had directed a question to her.

"W-what?"

"Mrs. Gullone asked if you have other friends your age in the neighborhood," Mother told her.

"No," Lynn said firmly, determined to protect Mouse. Again Mother stared at her hard.

"Lynn . . ." she said.

"I'm the only one who lives on our hill," Lynn said stubbornly.

"The hill, yes, but surely, with a school close by . . ." began the old lady.

Mother answered hurriedly: "The girls around here are in junior high now, and very busy. They have so many activities and hobbies, I hardly see much of Lynn and her friends myself."

"A pity," sighed Mrs. Gullone. "Elnora had a fondness for children. She never had any of her own, you know, and—"

"Then how could she have a grandson?" Lynn demanded.

Mrs. Gullone's eyes narrowed, and again she seemed to be reading Lynn's face like a fortune-teller.

"Eh? What's that?"

"A boy came to visit her a year ago from Michigan, and she told us he was her grandson."

"Perhaps you misunderstood."

"I understood perfectly, Mrs. Gullone."

"Lynn!" said Mother sharply.

There was silence in the room for a moment. Then

Mrs. Gullone's face brightened. "You see, *Mr.* Tuggle had a grown child of his own when he and Elnora were married. And it must have been the son of *that* child who came to visit. Her grandson by marriage, you see. Eh? There's my teakettle whistling away. Now we shall have a spot of tea to warm us." The old woman got up and left the room.

"You're being very rude, you know," Mother said to Lynn.

"Mom, doesn't it bother you that she looks so much like Mrs. Tuggle? That she rebuilt her house exactly the same, and even has the same kind of furniture?"

"They *were* sisters, you know."

"Yet she didn't even know that Mrs. Tuggle had a grandson? *I* think—" Lynn stopped as Mrs. Gullone came back with a teapot and cups on a tray. What Lynn thought was that this was not Mrs. Gullone but Mrs. Tuggle, who had forgotten she had once tried to pass her brother off as her grandson. Where the boy was now, Lynn didn't know, but she didn't think it was Michigan. Somewhere in this very neighborhood, probably, but as what, she wasn't sure.

Mrs. Gullone was talking again: "It was because Elnora had no child of her own that she was so attached to our brother, and a sad, sad story that was." The elderly woman went about distributing dessert plates. "She and her husband brought the boy with them when they came to the United States. Like a son he was to her. She watched him grow, start school, she wrote to me—watched him learn to ride a bike. And then one day he was gone. Disappeared so sudden it was like the bogles or hobyahs had carried him off, and people saw naught of him for two days. Then, of a Friday, Mr. Tuggle went down to the creek—'twas like a river then—and found the body floating facedown."

"Who killed him?" Lynn asked.

"Lynn, really!" said her mother, frowning now.

The old woman cocked her head, eyes mere slits as she studied Lynn. "Why, no one killed him, child! 'Twas an accident, but how, we'll never know." She poured the tea into three cups and passed one to Mrs. Morley, who took a polite sip and set it down again. When Lynn received hers, she put it down without tasting it at all.

"Where was your brother buried?" Lynn would not be stopped.

"That I don't know. I was too grieved to ask. He was gone, and it mattered not to me where he was buried."

She had covered for herself very nicely, Lynn thought. If she'd said that he was buried in the old cemetery, Lynn would have told her that the body found in that grave was not that of a boy at all, but rather that of a woman who had once suspected Mrs. Tuggle of witchcraft.

Lynn sat silently, wondering what she could do or say next to draw the old woman out, force her to reveal something that only Mrs. Tuggle could have known. The room seemed enormously larger and darker than it was when she and her mother had first entered. And even though Lynn herself had watched the house being built, it still seemed old. *Smelled* old, though perhaps it was the furniture and curtains. Old and strangely alive, as though even the figures on the wallpaper were watching.

"Drownings do happen, you see," Mrs. Gullone began again, "especially when the water is high. People get careless." She was directing the conversation to Mother now, as if to keep Lynn out of it. "There's a story we tell in England, that happened once in the North Country, I heard. 'Twas a girl, a wee one of three. She slipped out one night in the marsh, and a bad time it was, because the copse was all in bogs then, great pools of dark water, so they said, and creeping rivulets of green water, and squishy mools, which sank if ever you stepped on them."

The hair on the back of Lynn's neck seemed to rise up off her skin. This was exactly the same story Mrs. Tuggle had once told her and Mouse. Mother, however, listened raptly, like a child.

"They sent three men to seek her out," Mrs. Gullone continued, "and each of the three put a stone in his mouth and a hazel twig in his hand, and he vows not to say a word till he's home safe again.

"Well, they went along and went along, and the moon lit up the bog pools. There were shadows here and shadows there, waving rushes and trembling mools, and great black trees all twisted and bent. And sudden they came upon a box, half hidden it was, like a coffin, you know. And one of them up and forgets and speaks out loud, and when the others heard him talk, they up and ran home to get away from the quicks and the things that dwelt there. The middlin' man, he sees what he's done, so he thinks, 'Well, I'm done for it now,' so he might as well open the coffin anyway. So he pulls and he tugs and pushes, and finally the lid tumbles off, and there's naught inside but the little girl's fingers and toes. And some say if he hadn't spoken aloud, 'twould have been the whole girl herself ready to come home."

Mother gave a nervous laugh. "Now that's some story, Mrs. Gullone!"

Lynn sat absolutely speechless. She formed words with her mouth—making her tongue move, her teeth separate: "And what do *you* think, Mrs. Gullone?"

"Me, child?"

"About whether, if the man hadn't spoken aloud, they would have got the girl back whole? Was it witchcraft, do you think?"

Again the gold tooth gleamed from the back of her mouth as the old woman's lips stretched into a smile. "Well now, it could all be superstition."

"I'm wondering what *you* think." Lynn was amazed at her own boldness, especially in front of her mother who had taught her better manners than that.

"I'm thinking that there are some who meddle in things that aren't their business," the old woman said, and this time her eyes were on Lynn directly.

Mrs. Morley leaned forward and looked at her watch. "Well! I think we should be getting home, Lynn." And then, to Mrs. Gullone, she said, "I hope

you'll find Indiana to your liking. It always surprised me that someone from the Isle of Man would
come all the way here to make a home. First Elnora,
now you."

Mrs. Gullone simply shrugged it off. "Who's to
say where the heart calls home?" she answered, and
then, to Lynn, who was still staring: "You're wondering why both Elnora and I have one gray eye and
one green one. It's in the family—inherited from
our mother. When Elnora lost an eye as a child, she
had it replaced with the same color—a green one.
And even that, I'm told, must have been destroyed
in the fire along with her."

Her eyes studied Lynn more intently still, as
though she had almost asked a question. Was it
possible, Lynn wondered, that the woman *didn't*
know that the eye had survived? Or did she know
that it had, and this was what had drawn her here?
Perhaps both she and her sister were witches, and
she thought that if she were to rebuild Elnora's
house over the ashes of her old one, she might,
somehow, add her sister's power to her own.

Mrs. Gullone walked them to the door and again
Lynn was amazed at how quick and sturdy the old
woman's steps were, even though her back and
shoulders were bent. Like Mrs. Tuggle exactly.
There was strength in those hands as she opened the
door, and as Mrs. Morley said good-bye, Mrs. Gullone's face seemed made of steel—the jaws, the
chin, the nose, the teeth—as though she were age-
less and not even a fire could destroy her for long.

Lynn's mother said nothing until they were past

the thorn apple tree. Then she murmured, "If I didn't know better, I would have sworn that was Elnora herself. The resemblance almost took my breath away. I never saw sisters who looked so much alike."

"That's what I was thinking," Lynn said cautiously.

"I guess I can understand how she might want to rebuild her sister's house. Maybe she lost a husband, too, and this seemed a good way to make a new beginning. I guess . . ." She took a few more steps before she put her feelings into words. "I wish I felt more comfortable with her."

"Yeah, I know what you mean," Lynn admitted. And then, because she had an opening, "Dad doesn't want us to come up here at all."

"Why not?"

Lynn tried to appear casual. "Oh, I don't know. Maybe because of all that happened at Mrs. Tuggle's. You know. The fire and everything. He just said he'd rather we didn't come up here." She wondered if she'd said too much. She had, in fact, used the *W* word back at Mrs. Gullone's—actually said the word *witchcraft* in Mother's presence, and Mother hadn't collapsed or anything. She stole a quick look.

But Mother walked on hurriedly. "Well, your father didn't say anything to me about it, and he certainly can't object to a neighborly visit. It's the least we can do to welcome a new person on the street."

"But just for Dad's sake, let's not come up here

again," Lynn said. She hoped that would be the end of it. And she was surprised at her mother's reaction.

"I'm a grown woman, Lynn. If your father wants to tell me something, he can tell me himself." Her voice was sharper than Lynn had heard it for some time. "He doesn't need to do it through you. I intend to go and do whatever seems best to me. End of conversation."

Lynn's chest felt even colder than it had inside the house. Did this mean that there was some kind of trouble between her parents? That they, like the Beasleys, might separate? She had had misgivings about visiting the house on the hill as she'd gone up there with her mother, but now, going down, Lynn discovered that she felt even worse.

chapter five

"Lynn and I paid a visit to our new neighbor this afternoon," said Mother, placing a large bowl of chicken salad on the dining room table.

Her words seemed to bob about the room, refusing to settle down. Everyone tensed, except Stevie, who was reaching for a cinnamon roll.

"The new house?" Judith asked, staring.

Mother unfolded her napkin and spread it over her lap. "Yes, and it turns out that the occupant is Mrs. Tuggle's sister—a Mrs. Gullone. She evidently inherited the property and decided to rebuild the house just the way it was."

Lynn picked up her fork, but only toyed with her chicken salad. She could feel her father's eyes on her from across the table. *No secrets*, she reminded herself. *Keep everything out in the open.*

"Mom asked me if I'd go with her to help carry some food up," she told her father without waiting to be asked. "I didn't think you'd want her to go up there alone."

Stevie, who was digging the raisins out of the crevices of his cinnamon bun, looked up. "Why not?"

Lynn let her father answer.

"Because it doesn't seem like a very good idea to go inside people's houses until you know them well," he said.

"You went in*side*?" Judith asked, looking from Lynn to her mother and back again.

"Of course we went inside," said Mother. "She invited us. You don't just take someone food and walk off. You've got to be neighborly."

It seemed to Lynn that the dinner conversation continued in fits and starts. Questions were cautious and answers were wary.

"What's she like?" Judith asked, directing her question to Lynn this time.

"She looks exactly like Mrs. Tuggle," Lynn said, determined to stick to the truth. "She's short and thin and strong, and her shoulders are bony. She has a gold tooth in the exact same place that Mrs. Tuggle did, and one eye is green, the other gray."

Judith gasped, but Lynn plunged on: "If I'd met her on the street, I would have sworn she was Mrs. Tuggle herself."

Mr. Morley put down his fork. "Her name is Greta Gullone, and a firm in England drew up the bill of sale. I looked it up at the courthouse."

Everyone stared. So *this* was the information Dad was keeping to himself, Lynn thought: another woman coming from England. No wonder he had seemed so distracted lately. He was worried as much as any of them. A great relief washed over her. A worried father she could stand. A bewitched father, she could not.

"Well, if you already know so much about her,

Richard, she's hardly a total stranger," Mother retorted.

Forks clinked. Glasses were lifted to lips, then clunked again on the table.

"Let's be cautious; that's all I'm saying," said Father.

"Well, *I* say let's talk about something else," Stevie suggested. "This is boring."

Mother smiled then. "Okay, sweetie, what do you want to talk about?"

"Rabbits. I saw a big gray rabbit out in the yard and the next time it comes, I want to feed it something."

"It's probably the same one Lynn and I saw from the window one night," Judith told him. "I think it's a wild rabbit, Stevie. It would be hard to tame."

"But if I see it again, can I feed it?" Stevie persisted.

"You might put some lettuce out in back sometime, and if it's gone the next morning, you'll know the rabbit was by," Mother said.

It was later, when Mother was upstairs seeing Stevie to bed, and Lynn and Judith were clearing the kitchen, that Father came out and leaned against the door frame.

"Lynn, I thought I made it clear that I didn't want you going up to that house."

Lynn turned, a clutch of forks in her hand. "What should I have done, Dad? When I got home from school, Mom had the food ready to go. It sure wasn't my idea."

"What happened up there?"

"Just like Mom said, Mrs. Gullone invited us in. She made some tea. Mom drank a couple sips, I didn't drink any. Mrs. Gullone told us she was Mrs. Tuggle's sister, and asked if I had any friends my age around here. I said no, I didn't have any friends up here on the hill. I don't want her trying to lure Mouse up there or anything."

Mr. Morley ran one hand thoughtfully through his hair. "Did your mother say she'd be back? Make plans to see her again?"

"No. If you want the truth, I think Mom thought it was as creepy up there as I did. She told me afterward that she felt uncomfortable with Mrs. Gullone."

"Well, that's good. Now that she's made a neighborly gesture, perhaps she won't feel obliged to do more."

Judith began sorting the silverware from the basket to the drawer. "What are you afraid will happen if she *does* go back, Dad?"

"I worry that she'll get involved in something she can't cope with. She was drawn to that house before, and I'm afraid she might be drawn up there again. This whole business of rebuilding that house, just as it was, seems awfully strange to me. I found out a month ago that a firm in England was handling the sale, and I've been uneasy. And now, to find out that the woman is Mrs. Tuggle's sister . . . Mrs. Gullone's not been here more than a few days, and already your mother's up there."

"Dad, she'd be up there no matter who moved in; that's just the way she is."

"I suppose so."

"And if she *does* want to go up there, what do you want me to do?" Lynn asked. "Not go with her? Try to stop her?"

Mr. Morley shrugged as Mother's footsteps sounded on the stairs. "Just tell me everything that goes on," he said. "We'll handle it one day at a time."

What Lynn felt like was a spy, and she didn't care for it. Felt as though she had to report everything her mother did. But Dad was worried. They were all worried. What else could they do?

Mr. Morley left the room, and Judith cleared off the kitchen counter. Lynn watched the way her cloth made jagged sweeps around the flour and sugar containers. "Maybe we should just move," Judith said finally.

"Why?"

The voice startled them both, and Lynn and Judith turned to see Mother standing just inside the kitchen door.

"Why should we move? Have I missed something?"

Judith gave a quick laugh. "To a town where there are more boys," she joked. "Good-looking boys, I mean."

Mother smiled. "There are always good-looking boys around; keep your eyes open, that's all."

And that was another thing Lynn hated. Lying to Mother the way they did.

She got a phone call from Marjorie later.

"Guess what?" came Mouse's voice. "I got a letter from Mom. A long one."

"You did?" Lynn was glad for any kind of good news, even if it didn't involve her. "What did she say?"

"Lots." Mouse didn't sound particularly happy. "It . . . it wasn't what I wanted to hear, Lynn, but I guess I needed to know it. I guess I needed Mom to say it so I could stop hoping."

It *wasn't* good news, then.

"Say what?"

"That she's not coming back. That she knows how much I want her and Dad to live together again, but she just can't. She says that as much as she misses me, she just isn't happy with Dad, that they're both too different to get along, and she hopes that some-day I'll understand. That I'll agree she did the right thing. For her, anyway."

What Lynn realized this time was that Mouse wasn't crying. She wasn't happy, and there was a sad, flat sound to her voice, but maybe a bit of relief, too.

"Did she say any more about your visiting her?" Lynn asked gently.

"She said she wants me to come back as soon as she has a regular job. She's working part-time now, but when she gets her life in order, she wants me to visit again and stay longer."

"Well, *that* much is good," Lynn said.

"Yeah. Maybe I knew this all along, Lynn—that she wasn't coming back. But I couldn't believe it until she said it herself. It doesn't stop the wanting, though."

"Of course not, Mouse. Knowing and wanting are two different things."

For a long time that night, Lynn thought about her own parents. Worried about them. Finally she told herself that if it ever seemed to her that *they* weren't getting along—that they were just too different to be happy together—she would suggest that they both go to Dr. Long for counseling. And having something definite she could suggest if she *did* see trouble, she finally fell asleep.

Mrs. Morley did not mention Greta Gullone for the next few days. Lynn told Mouse what they had found out about the old woman, but Mother did not talk about her at all. In some ways, Lynn felt, Mother was retreating back into the silence that had overtaken her after Mrs. Tuggle's house burned to the ground. There were many times Lynn entered the room to find her staring off into space. Yet she did this a lot when she was writing a new book, so that wasn't too unusual. And when she was around the family, she seemed interested in their activities, and joined in the conversation at mealtime. When she wasn't working on her manuscript, she kept busy making applesauce or sewing a quilt she had started recently.

The problem that consumed Lynn was whether or not it was possible that Mrs. Tuggle had *not* died in the fire, and had indeed come back. Yet even as she considered it, it seemed just too preposterous to take seriously. She tried to re-create those last terrifying moments of the fire, when she and her mother had barely managed to crawl out the window onto the upper porch and make their way down the side stairs in the smoke, before the whole house erupted in flames. She still wondered if Mrs. Tuggle could possibly have crawled out behind them and got away.

No, Lynn felt sure of it. She would have heard her coming, seen her. In fact, she had a dim memory of the old woman framed in the upstairs window as she glanced back at the burning house. And then, of course, there was the green glass eye found in the rubble. Lynn had no other choice but to believe that Greta Gullone and Elnora Tuggle were, as Mrs. Gullone said, sisters.

Kirsten's birthday party was on Saturday, and Mouse came to the Morleys' early to let Judith fix her hair. Judith washed it for her and showed her how to curl the ends under, then lent her a red sweater with black sheep on it to wear with her jeans.

The weather was crisp and cool, with leaves beginning to fall, and when Lynn and Mouse walked down the hill, then over five blocks to Kirsten's, they played a game of stepping only on leaves as they went, hopping and skipping from one patch to another.

Charlotte Ann and Betty were there at the party with other girls from seventh grade, sitting out on the porch railing blowing soap bubbles out of a large ring that Kirsten had received as a present. They greeted Lynn and Mouse with a shower of bubbles as the two came up the walk.

"Can you *believe* that assignment Mr. Esselrod gave us in English?" Betty asked as Lynn stepped up on the porch. "When you get to junior high, the teachers think that their subject is the only one you've got—that nobody else ever gives homework but them."

"I know," said Lynn. "I worked on it some last night. Happy birthday, Kirsten!" She handed Kirsten a gift that she and Mouse had bought together, and the girls trooped inside when the last of the guests arrived.

It was good to have a lot of friends, Lynn was thinking as they all sat around the table, savoring the chocolate ice cream and fudge cake while Kirsten opened the rest of her gifts.

Nobody mentioned the fire. There was no talk of the witch weed that Lynn had burned down at the creek, or the gulls that had been found in Cowden's Creek with their necks broken and twisted. No talk at all of anything except birthdays and school and the junior high play that was coming up in November.

Kirsten's mother was something like a schoolteacher, because she had a whole list of games for the girls to play, beginning with a treasure hunt for party trinkets hidden about the house, and ending at last with paper and pencil games, and still more ice cream around the table.

The game Lynn liked best was a scrambled-word game in which the girls were given a list of words, each of them having to do with birthdays. The winner would be whichever girl could unscramble them first, and Lynn was surprised that she was the winner. Words like *akec* (cake); *trepness* (presents); *sadlenc* (candles); *blotceraine* (celebration). Lynn's prize was a little Viking ship.

"Maybe we could have a slumber party at my house sometime," Betty said. "I'm going to have a zillion problems with math this year, I can tell. Maybe we could do homework together."

Lynn enjoyed the feeling of being included.

She and Mouse walked home together after the party, Marjorie's hair still fresh and bouncy.

"You looked great at the party, Mouse," Lynn said. "That's a good way to fix your hair."

"Maybe the next time I visit Mom, Judith could do it for me again."

Lynn stopped suddenly and grabbed Marjorie's arm. "Look." There, just this side of the hedge, was the large gray rabbit. It sat like a statue, and for a moment Lynn thought it was made of ceramic. Then, as she took a cautious step forward, she saw its ears move ever so slightly. It sat with its left eye turned directly toward the girls, and for a time it seemed that this was all that was alive about it— the large dark eye—watching, staring.

"Stevie wants to feed it things," Lynn said. "I don't know . . ."

"You don't know what?"

Lynn shrugged. "I don't know *what* I don't know."

"You're weird, Lynn."

"I suppose."

Helping Mother make the salad for dinner, Lynn told her about the party.

"I think it's wonderful that you and Mouse have made up with those girls," Mother said. "You have a lot of good times ahead."

"I hope so."

Lynn had brought home with her the list of words that had won her a prize at the party, and when she went to her room later, settled down on her bed to look them over. The neat thing about the game was that the mixed-up letters themselves seemed to form words of sorts.

She wrote her own name on the paper to figure out a way to make the letters spell something else, and smiled when she rearranged them to say *Normy Nelly*.

She tried Mouse's next: *Marjorie Beasley = Sorry Jaime Leabe*.

Lynn didn't know why, but she found her pencil writing down the new neighbor's name on her sheet of paper. *Greta Gullone*. She tried this combination, then that.

And then her heart began to beat faster. Her fingers scribbled, her eyes opened wide, and she stared. *Greta Gullone = Elnora Tuggle*.

chapter six

"Mouse." Lynn could hear music in the background and knew that Marjorie was watching TV. "Did you finish that English assignment?"

"About five minutes ago."

"Then listen," Lynn said over the phone. "I want you to do something. Get a pencil and paper."

"You want me to do *yours.*"

"No."

Lynn heard Mouse putting the receiver down, footsteps, and then Marjorie's voice again. "Okay. Now what?"

"Write 'Greta Gullone.'" Lynn spelled out the last name for her. "Pretend it's one of those mixed-up words in that game we played at Kirsten's, and see what you get. Call me back."

She sat by the phone in the hallway and waited. Judith was in the music room playing a song she was singing with the high school chorus. Stevie and Dad were out in the kitchen making popcorn, and Mother was curled up at one end of the couch with her manuscript. Why couldn't life always be like this? Lynn wondered. If they just *totally* ignored Mrs. Gullone and everything connected with her, was it possible they could wear her out? Keep

the witchcraft from taking over? Make it pass over
onto . . .

Lynn swallowed. She had started to think, . . .
onto someone else. But was that fair? When you
knew there was something wrong, something evil,
could you just ignore it as long as it didn't affect
you? Lynn already knew the answer.

The phone rang.

"Here's what I've got, Lynn. 'One great gull.' "

"Do it again, Mouse, and this time look for someone else's name."

"Someone we know?"

"Yes."

It was only about two minutes before the phone
rang again: Mouse's voice, soft and shaky: "Elnora
Tuggle."

"Right."

"Oh, Lordy!"

There was complete silence for a while, neither of
them quite knowing what to say.

"You know," Mouse said at last, "if Mrs. Tuggle
and Mrs. Gullone were sisters, maybe the letters of
their names make up the names of their parents or
something. I mean, some parents do things like
that—name all their kids the same somehow."

"Uh-uh. Think about it, Mouse. 'Tuggle' was
Elnora's *married* name. 'Gullone' is supposed to be a
married name too."

"Are you going to tell your father?"

"He'll say it's all coincidence. I'll tell Judith
first—see what she says."

But I don't think it's coincidence, Lynn wrote in

her journal that night. *If there were letters left over, maybe. But that the exact number of letters in "Greta Gullone" should also spell "Elnora Tuggle" is just too spooky to be accidental.*

"What are you doing?" Judith asked when she came up to the bedroom later.

"Trying to figure out something," Lynn said. "Come here a minute."

Lynn's sister came over and looked at the paper Lynn handed her, on which she had crossed off the letters in one name to make the other.

Judith studied it a moment, and then, her eyes widening, sat down slowly on the edge of the bed. "How did you figure this out?"

Lynn explained about the game they had played at Kirsten's party, and how she was just fooling around with names when she discovered this. "Judith," she said, "I think that Mrs. Gullone *is* Mrs. Tuggle. I really do. I wish you'd seen her. They look *exactly* alike. I'm sure Mom thinks so too. She just doesn't let on."

Judith still sat with one hand over her mouth. "But how . . . ?"

"I don't know."

"Mom's not going up there again, is she?"

"She hasn't said."

"Listen. That book that was in Mr. Beasley's bookstore. The one you and Mouse were reading. Does it explain how you can tell if a person really is a witch?"

"I don't know. I don't think I've looked for that."

"Well, get it and let's check."

"Where's Mom?"

"In the living room, I think."

"You go down and start a conversation with her to make sure she stays there, and I'll go get *Spells and Potions* and bring it up here."

Judith went down to the first floor and Lynn, listening on the landing, waited until she heard her voice talking with Mother. Then she went into her parents' bedroom, retrieved the sack from under the bed, and took it up to the third-floor bedroom. It was over the summer, when the girls from school had begun going to Mr. Beasley's bookstore to read *Spells and Potions*, that Mr. Beasley sold the rare book to Mr. Morley for one dollar, just to get it out of the store and to say it had been sold. The understanding was, of course, that he could buy it back anytime he liked. Father kept it hidden under the bed, and it was there Lynn had found it once when she was cleaning.

Judith came up a little later, and the girls carefully turned the yellowed, crumbling pages to see if there was any section about how you could tell a witch from an ordinary person. It was a difficult search, for there was no index, and even the headings weren't alphabetical. Finally, however, Lynn came across two pages that had been stuck together, and there, inside, was a section titled, "Discerning a Witch." Judith read it aloud while Lynn lay on her back, staring up at the shadows on the ceiling, remembering the night the bat had got into the room and lured her out into the storm, almost into the waters of Cowden's Creek.

" 'Discerning a witch,' " Judith began. " 'Of great importance to those who would protect themselves from the likes of witchcraft is how one may discern a witch from those women who, though having the appearance and demeanour of hags, may possess a goodly heart and kind intentions toward their neighbours. For there is many an old woman who, though her back is bent, her skin shriveled, and her chin covered with hairs, may be a lonely widow with a cat for company, and it would be a great injustice should the village rise up against her and call her witch.' "

Judith stopped reading as Mother's voice sounded below, but then they heard her talking to Stevie. Judith went on:

" 'Indeed, appearance is not a factor to be considered, for there have been those women and girls, young in age and fair in both face and form, who have, in their hearts, naught but evil, and who possess the power to inflict harm upon neighbours, flock, and cattle.' "

Lynn found herself rubbing her arms as though the house were freezing.

" 'Whereas any one of the following traits may be found in good-hearted women, several abiding in one woman alone would be cause for suspicion, and if a single woman were to possess them all, one may be sure indeed that she has within her the power and talent for witchcraft.' "

"What are they?" Lynn asked. "The traits?"

"Shhh." Judith paused a moment, listening for Mother's voice in Stevie's room. There was no sound at all, but then the girls heard noises in the kitchen far below, their parents' voices, and Judith continued reading:

" 'It is often thought that a witch learns her art from her mother or some other woman of her acquaintance, and so passes it on to children of her own or to those unsuspecting young lads and lasses in her village. Therefore, to discern whether a woman be a witch, pay close attention to her eyes, for a witch scarcely takes her eyes from you; she stares with a gaze that is cold as ice. Her fingernails are more like claws, and her touch, if it does not scratch the skin, would be cold as winter's snows; a witch avoids salt, the sign of the cross, and is unable to weep. It is also believed that somewhere upon a witch's body is a mark that—' "

"Judith! Lynn!"

Judith closed the book quickly as Mother called them from the stairs.

"There's a wonderful program on Russia just beginning. I really think you ought to watch it."

"Coming!" Judith said, and then, to Lynn: "I'll go down first while you put the book away."

Sunday afternoon was windy and cool, with dark clouds blowing in from the north. Lynn and Mouse rode their bikes around the downtown area, but all stores except one restaurant were closed. The spray from the fountain at the center of town blew against them as the wind gusted, and as soon as the temperature dropped to freezing, the fountain would be shut off for the winter.

It had always seemed to Lynn that this first week of the new month, the edge of October, brought with it the dark moodiness of the months to come, and was not surprised to find that, even without thinking about it, she was leading the way through the iron gates of the old cemetery to their favorite talking place.

She parked her bike and sat down thoughtfully on the fallen tombstone of Mrs. Elfreda Lewis, using the upright tombstone of Mr. Lewis as a backrest. Mouse, as usual, took the open marble book, held between two angels, whose lidless eyes looked either down on the book or off into space. Lynn was never quite sure.

"That's what we found out," Lynn said, after telling Marjorie what the book had said. "I don't know if Mrs. Gullone has a mark somewhere on her body or if she never weeps, but I *do* know that her fingers feel like chicken feet, and she almost never takes her eyes off you when you come to visit. Mrs. Tuggle was the same way. Mouse, I'm positive . . . well, I'm sure . . . I mean, I really, truly believe that Mrs. Gullone is Mrs. Tuggle."

"But how *could* she be?"

"I don't know. That's the part I haven't figured out."

"Have you talked with your dad about it?"

"No."

"We promised, you know. No more secrets."

"Let's tell yours, just for practice."

The tombstones were cold anyway, so the girls got on their bikes again and rode back through the business district, down a side street, and into the Beasleys' front yard.

Marjorie's father always seemed like a big gentle bear to Lynn. He was slightly on the plump side, with a thick, bushy mustache. Lynn used to wonder if perhaps the mustache could have driven Mrs. Beasley away, but now she knew life was more complicated than that. It was probably not one thing at all, but lots of little things. And Mouse, she felt sure, was not one of the "things" responsible for their breakup.

"Hi, girls," Mr. Beasley said. He was sitting in his stocking feet, working the Sunday crossword puzzle, and had on an old brown sweater that had been buttoned wrong at the bottom. He looked all right when he was at the bookstore, but he didn't much care how he dressed at home.

"Hi, Dad. Lynn wants to talk with you," Mouse said, taking off her sweat jacket.

Lynn would have preferred Mouse to say, "We want to talk with you." But it was Lynn, after all, who had been to Mrs. Gullone's, not Marjorie, so it was up to Lynn to do the talking.

Mr. Beasley finished writing down the word he was working on, then laid the paper in his lap. "What's up?"

"I know this sounds weird . . ." Lynn began.

Why was it that no matter how emphatically adults told you to come to them with problems, pleaded with you, *begged* you, even, to tell them whatever was on your mind, there were things they didn't want to know about, no matter what. Lynn had not even mentioned Mrs. Tuggle yet. She had not even said the words *Greta Gullone*. All she had said was "I know this sounds weird . . ." and she could tell by the slight sag of Mr. Beasley's mustache at the ends, and the almost imperceptible rise of his shoulders, that whatever Lynn was about to tell him was not going to make him happy.

Lynn cleared her throat and tried again. "Has Dad told you who moved into Mrs. Tuggle's house? I mean, the house that was built over the old one?"

Mr. Beasley rested his arms on top of his round stomach. "Yes. He and Dr. Long and I had a talk about it the other day. It's a Mrs. Greta Gullone, from England, and she's evidently Mrs. Tuggle's sister. Do you see something unusual—something sinister or strange—about that, Lynn?"

Well, if *they* didn't think it was strange, why had they had a talk about it? Lynn wondered.

"Yes," she said simply.

"Why? The property goes to the surviving relatives, who, in this case, seem to be only one: Greta Gullone."

"Mrs. Tuggle supposedly had a grandson in Michigan," Lynn said.

"Really? Well, even so, I imagine the house would go to her sister."

"Have you met her?"

"No."

Lynn looked him right in the eye. "Mr. Beasley, Mrs. Gullone looks exactly like Mrs. Tuggle. Same height, same weight, same hair, same walk. She even has a gold tooth exactly where Mrs. Tuggle had one."

"Lynn . . ."

"More than that, though, the letters of each name spell the name of the other one too."

"What do you mean?"

"She means that the twelve letters of 'Greta Gullone' are the same letters that spell 'Elnora Tuggle,' " Mouse told him.

"Now, how in the world did you figure that out?"

"It was like a game we played at a birthday party. I was just fooling around with the letters, and that's what I discovered," said Lynn.

"It's a coincidence! If you had their middle names as well, it probably wouldn't work out at all. And even if it did, it's not the kind of evidence that would hold up in court. I'm sure your dad would agree."

Lynn had to make him understand: "I'm positive that Mrs. Gullone is Mrs. Tuggle."

"Lynn, Lynn, Lynn . . . !" Mr. Beasley tipped back his head, bemused. "Now let's be sensible, girl. You saw her house burn to the ground, her inside at the window. Stevie found the glass eye."

"Did anyone find her bones, Mr. Beasley?"

"No, not that I know of. But in the terrible heat of such a fire . . ."

"Teeth?"

"No . . ."

"Was a death report ever filed?"

"It's assumed she's dead, Lynn. Where else would she be? She was an old woman. Do you think she jumped out a second-story window, sailed off on a broomstick, and has been living in the woods somewhere?" And then he apologized. "I'm sorry. I didn't mean to sound sarcastic. How do *you* explain it?"

"I don't. I can't. But Dad says that when you don't understand something, you don't have to make up explanations. You can just say, 'I don't know.' "

"Fair enough."

"So all I'm saying is that I think Mrs. Gullone and Mrs. Tuggle are the same person, and I think something terrible might happen," Lynn said determinedly.

"What does your dad think?"

"I haven't told him yet."

"But you will."

"Yes."

"I'll ride home with you," Mouse said when Lynn got up to leave, and when they were out on the porch, she said, "He didn't think much of that letter game. Are you going to tell your dad about it?"

"No, because he'd say the same thing—that it doesn't *prove* anything. It's weird and stupid," Lynn said discouragingly.

They had reached the hill and, as always, rode partway up, then walked their bikes the rest of the way. The clouds were getting darker, making the late afternoon seem almost evening.

They had just reached the sycamore tree in a neighbor's yard when they heard footsteps coming up behind them, and when Lynn turned, she almost let go of the handlebars, for there was Mrs.

Gullone—small, thin, and slightly bent—walking with a brisk step.

Lynn quickly moved to one side to let her pass, but the woman slowed.

"Ah! The girlies!" she said. "Just the ones to help an old woman carry her black walnuts home. The bag gets heavier each step I take. 'Tis though a bogle itself jumped in my sack, and my arms will soon give out." Without waiting for an answer, she set the old burlap bag into the basket of Marjorie's bike.

Lynn stared, stupefied. There was no way in the world Mouse could refuse to help an old woman carry a heavy bundle. Even if it had been Lynn's basket into which the woman had dumped it, and after the rudeness Lynn had shown Mrs. Gullone, she still could not imagine herself saying "No, carry it yourself."

And because Mouse stood as though frozen, her lips slightly parted, a look of horror on her face, Lynn said, "We'll carry it as far as your door, Mrs. Gullone," and the caravan set off again. Greta Gullone walked just ahead, a crooked smile on her face.

chapter seven

If, as they passed her own house, Lynn decided, she saw anyone outside—Mother or Dad or Judith—she would call out that they were helping Mrs. Gullone carry a bag of black walnuts and ask someone to come along. The presence of one of her parents or even Judith would surely prevent the old woman from trying something evil.

"I've a fondness for black walnuts, that I do," Mrs. Gullone said. "When I walked down to the store the first day I was here, I saw the black walnut tree just beyond, near the road to the cemetery. I like a good walk, so I set out this afternoon with my bag, and now I've a hard job ahead of me getting the sweet meats out of the shells."

Lynn tried to keep her imagination in check as she glanced over at the large burlap sack that filled all of Marjorie's bike basket and even bulged out over the top. How did they know there were really walnuts in there? What if they were bones, human bones? What was that dreadful story Mrs. Gullone had told her and Mother about a little girl who disappeared one night, and all that was found of her were her fingers and toes? Somehow she thought of Stevie again, and her heart thumped painfully.

"W-what do you do with black walnuts?" Mouse asked, ever the polite one. Lynn's aim was to simply deliver the old woman and her sack to the front door as quickly as possible, but Mouse felt obliged to make conversation.

"Why, tea cakes, my dear. I make tea cakes and cookies. You shall come to my house for cake and tea, for all your help in getting a poor woman and her sack up the hill."

It didn't fool Lynn for a moment. If Mrs. Gullone had energy enough to walk all the way into town and then some—over to the road near the cemetery, in fact—it didn't seem likely she needed help getting the last block up the hill. And if she was here without a car and was new in town, how did she even know there was a cemetery up there? Again, the heart-pounding, like a drumbeat, inside Lynn's chest.

She decided that if she were going to get any information at all about Mrs. Gullone, however, she had better be polite about it, so she said, "I think we were all surprised that you rebuilt such a large house for just one person."

"Eh?" Mrs. Gullone seemed to be thinking that over a bit. "Well, 'twas guilt, perhaps. Elnora always wanted me to come live with her here, and 'twas first one thing, then another, that kept me from coming. So when I got word, you see, that she had perished in the fire, I had to rebuild her house— the only thing left to do. A homage to her spirit, don't you know."

They had reached the long stretch of empty lot

between Mrs. Gullone's house and her nearest neighbor, and Lynn's uneasiness grew. There was no porch to run up on if they suddenly needed help; no doorbell to ring. The wind had picked up even stronger, and darkness was approaching faster than usual because of the coming storm.

"Besides," the old woman added, "I like a bit of company, that I do. I must have room for my visitors."

Lynn considered carefully what she would say next. Mouse had turned almost speechless, or perhaps she was concentrating too hard on keeping the sack of black walnuts upright. As they passed the thick grove of trees that separated Mrs. Gullone's property from the empty lot, Lynn said, "Some people wonder why your sister gave up living on the Isle of Man to come to the United States and settle in Indiana in the first place."

"*Do* they, now?" They had turned up the walk, past the branches of the thorn apple tree, and Mrs. Gullone reached into her pocket for the key. "*Who* wonders, dearie? You, I think. People move here, people move there. . . . Not much to wonder over now, is it?" And then, to Marjorie, "Just come inside and set that sack on my kitchen table, love."

"We'll have to hurry to make it back before it rains," Lynn said, helping to lift the heavy bag out of Marjorie's bike basket, and managing a peek inside. Walnuts, just like the woman said. Each holding a corner, she and Mouse dragged it up the steps. How Mrs. Gullone had carried it so far herself, Lynn couldn't imagine.

The brass knocker on the door, the ugly troll with the long tongue, seemed to mock Lynn as they stepped inside. Mrs. Gullone turned on a lamp in the hallway so that they could see their way to the kitchen.

Once in the kitchen, the old woman went swiftly to the sink and filled a small bowl with water. She half turned her body away from them, but Lynn and Mouse could see that she had thrust one finger in the bowl and was stirring it rapidly around and around, her lips moving silently. Lynn and Mouse headed for the front door.

By the time Lynn opened it, however, a sudden flash of lightning zigzagged across the sky, and the thunder—which had been only a low distant rumble before—crashed out of nowhere. Rain came slashing down.

Darn! Lynn said to herself. *Darn, darn, darn!* "We'll just stand out here on the porch until it's over," she told the old woman, but in the next instant, hailstones as large as marbles came pelting down, driven sideways onto the porch by the gusting wind, and there was nothing to be done but go back inside and wait until the storm was over.

Lynn glanced at her watch as the girls sat side by side on the velvet sofa. Ten minutes yet before dinner. It would be longer than that before her parents were worried enough to start calling around or go looking for her. Had anyone seen her and Mouse walking their bikes up the hill beside Mrs. Gullone? Would anyone have the slightest idea where they were?

"I think I should call home and tell Mom where I am," Lynn said aloud.

"I've no phone as yet, my girls. Too much to do in so short a time. And besides, who would I know to call? Who takes pity on a lonely old woman who likes nothing better than a spot of tea, some biscuits, and someone to share them with. I'll put the kettle on." She stood up and disappeared from the room.

Lynn grabbed Mouse by the arm. "We are *not* eating or drinking anything. *Promise* me that."

"But I'm hungry!"

"Mouse, *promise*!"

"What am I supposed to say, then, when she offers me something?"

"Just tell her you're feeling sick. You think you're going to throw up or something. She won't make you try to eat, I promise."

"She made it storm, you know."

Lynn looked at Mouse curiously. "How? You mean, her finger in that bowl of water?"

Mouse nodded. "I remember reading it. Witches can cause storms—even hurricanes—by making a whirlpool in a bowl of water and chanting something."

Off in the kitchen, the teakettle began to sing.

" 'Whistling kettle, tinkling bell, weave your web and spin your spell,' " Lynn murmured softly.

"Now then!" Mrs. Gullone came back in the room carrying a tray with some cups and a plate of cookies. "We'll let the tea steep a few minutes, and then it will warm us. By and by the rain will be over, and you shall go home with a warm stomach and an invitation to visit me again."

What if she *was* just a lonely old woman? Lynn thought. What if, as Elnora Tuggle's sister, she'd had no more idea what her sister had been up to than most of the other people in town? Maybe she had simply hurt her finger picking up walnuts and was soaking it a moment or two in a bowl of baking soda and water. Maybe it had nothing to do with the storm at all, and all she had said was true about feeling guilty she had not come earlier to live with her sister. Was Lynn being unfair to an old woman and far too suspicious? Or was she becoming ensnared in the net? Father was right about not wanting the girls up here alone.

"It smells very good," Lynn said politely, looking at the food before her, "but I'm not allowed to eat or drink anything before dinner." And when she saw Mouse eyeing the cookies, she said, "Mouse can't have any either."

"Mouse, eh? Now that's a strange name." Mrs. Gullone smiled. "Mouse and cat. Cat and mouse. So you can't eat anything before dinner? A pity." She helped herself to one of the cookies, which did look delicious. "I use only fresh cream and eggs and butter to make my biscuits, girls, and little curls of chocolate, enough to—"

Marjorie's hand shot out and picked up a cookie. "I can eat just one," she said, "but tea makes me sick."

"Just a biscuit, then," Mrs. Gullone crooned.

Lynn glared at Mouse, but Marjorie avoided her

eyes and, with a small smile of satisfaction, leaned back against the sofa, savoring a bite of pastry in her mouth. Outdoors, the hail which had stopped a few minutes earlier came again even harder, pounding against the windows—rat-a-tat-tat—and plunked on the roof. They sounded like golf balls.

"Stones that size might break the glass," Lynn commented.

"Aye, that they might," the old woman said. Despite the girls' refusal to drink tea, she poured them each a cup and let the steam rise in the air where it seemed to swirl in a cloud in front of their faces. Lynn caught its scent and waved it away with one hand.

"Some music, then!" Mrs. Gullone said gaily. "Some music to wait out the storm!" And as Lynn stared, she reached for a music box on the coffee table and set it in her lap.

"That's . . . that's Mrs. Tuggle's!" Lynn exclaimed.

"Ah, we each had one, you see," Mrs. Gullone said. "We did indeed. They were given us by our mother." And without waiting for an invitation to play, she grasped the handle on one side of the box, and a familiar melody filled the room. Mouse stopped chewing as the old woman sang the words:

> *"Sing of morning, sing of noon,*
> *Sing of evening's silver moon.*
> *Feel the darkness, touch the black,*
> *Hear the shadows whisper back."*

Lynn stood up. "It's time to go, Mouse."

"Don't like my song, eh?" Mrs. Gullone said. "Why, 'tis an old song sung by the women in Castletown. My mother taught it to us. Passed it down from woman to woman."

"Mouse!" Lynn said again.

Now Marjorie was sitting with her head tipped back, eyes closed, half a cookie in her hand, and Lynn could see that the steam from the untouched tea cup in front of her swirled right under her nose. She leaned over and shook her. "Mouse!"

Marjorie opened her eyes.

"We're going," Lynn said. "The hail has stopped, at least." She half expected Mrs. Gullone to dip her finger in her teacup and bring hailstones the size of basketballs. But the woman let them go.

"Do come back and help me crack the walnuts," she said. "I'll let you each take some home. 'Twas years, I'll wager, since your mothers baked you a black walnut cake."

Mouse did not answer and Lynn did not pause. They got up, went down the hallway, and the door closed after them. But Lynn could see eyes within the hollow eyes of the troll door knocker, staring out at them, watching. It was still raining lightly, but the downpour of fifteen minutes before had left large puddles on the sidewalk, along with a sprinkling of hailstones. Lynn guided Mouse over to their bikes.

"Mouse, are you crazy?" she scolded. "Sitting there eating her cookies, smelling her tea? This was exactly what happened the first time we ever went to Mrs. Tuggle's. You zonked out then."

"I just felt so wonderfully tired, Lynn. I could hear everything you were saying. I just didn't seem to care."

"That's what I thought." Lynn jerked Marjorie's bike up from the steps and waited till she was on it.

"Don't be mad, Lynn."

"I'm *not* mad! I'm scared! We've got this old lady who looks like Mrs. Tuggle, sounds like Mrs. Tuggle, living in the same kind of house, singing the same songs, and here we are, just asking for trouble. Mouse, we aren't going to let it happen again. We are *not* going to get involved. We *can't*! I'm going to tell Dad everything that happened."

They silently rode out of Mrs. Gullone's yard and into the street, the rain pattering down on their backs.

"I wish Mom was here," Mouse said softly, as the wheels of their bikes made a slick, whirring sound on the wet street.

"What does your mom have to do with it?"

"She used to give me tea and cookies. Well, cocoa anyway."

"Come up to our house and I'll give you all the tea and cocoa and cookies you want. I'll make you cakes! I'll make you lemonade! Just don't go back to Mrs. Gullone's!"

"I know. I'm not crazy enough to fall for that again. I'm just stating facts. I wish Mom was back."

"So do I, Mouse." Lynn's voice softened. "Really."

The family was halfway through dinner when Lynn came in, her jacket soaked through, hair dripping.

"Lynn, I was getting worried!" Mother said, irritation in her voice. "Where on earth have you been? Didn't you see it clouding up?"

"Mouse and I were riding around and thought we could make it home before the storm. But those hailstones came so fast and hard," Lynn said.

"The second time around they were huge. I've never seen any that big. I thought for a minute they were going to break a window," her father said. "Go dry off and sit down."

Lynn was glad she could get by with no other questions than that.

Mr. Morley had a meeting that evening, so Lynn put off telling him about what had happened. She went upstairs after dinner, took out her journal, and wrote in every detail so she wouldn't forget a thing, being careful to write *it seemed as though* when she wasn't really sure, or *I think* when she had no proof, yet stating what facts she *did* have as accurately as possible.

Judith had gone to a movie with some girlfriends, Stevie was in bed, and Lynn's mother was watching TV in the bedroom when Lynn stopped writing at last and went down to the kitchen for a dish of ice cream.

She had just scooped up a spoonful of rocky road and had added another of praline pecan when she heard the singing, so faint, at first she thought it was the TV on the next floor. But there was no mistaking the words:

"From the shadows of the pool,
Black as midnight, thick as gruel,
Come, my nymphs, and you shall be,
Silent images of me."

"No!" Lynn said, setting her bowl on the counter.

"Suck the honey from my lips,
Dance upon my fingertips.
When the darkness tolls the hour,
I shall have you in my power."

The singing was not coming from the back of the house, Lynn discovered, but from the front. She got up and walked toward the front door.

"Fast upon us, spirits all,
Listen for our whispered call.
Whistling kettle, tinkling bell,
Weave your web and spin your spell."

Lynn put her hand on the knob and opened the front door. She caught a glimpse of the large gray rabbit before it hopped away.

chapter eight

Bodily transfiguration. The words kept coming back to Lynn again and again. It was the only way she could explain the gray rabbit. The only way she could begin to explain Greta Gullone.

She could not go in her parents' bedroom now and get *Spells and Potions*, not with Mother there. But she was sure there was something in it about the ability of witches to transform themselves into animals of various sorts, or to transform their familiars from one animal to another, or to transform another person or another witch into some other shape entirely. *Dipping into water or milk is necessary before one can be transformed*, Mouse had told her once, reading from the book.

Twice Lynn had suspected Mrs. Tuggle of trying to prepare someone for later transfiguration. The first was that night a year or so ago when Mrs. Tuggle had been sitting the Morley children, and at supper, the old woman had taken Stevie's fingers, holding a biscuit, and dipped them into his milk, saying that nothing was better than biscuits and cream. Had Judith, who was then under Mrs. Tuggle's power, succeeded in getting Stevie out on the porch later, he might have been transformed into something else, and no one would have suspected, had they heard a shriek, that it was a small boy—not a mouse or a young possum—being carried off in the dead of night.

Another day, Lynn and Mouse had been down at Cowden's Creek—at the water's edge—and Mrs. Tuggle had appeared out of nowhere with her walking stick; she had brushed by Mouse so forcefully that she had shoved her into the water, then held out her stick to pull her back in, chanting words that Lynn could not understand.

Maybe Mrs. Gullone, dipping her fingers in a bowl of water that evening, had nothing at all to do with the storm, but had been preparing herself for transfiguration instead. Perhaps it was she who had come in the disguise of a rabbit, singing her strange song. If a witch has achieved her highest powers, Lynn had read, she has merely to dip her victim—or a part of herself—in water or milk and say, "I conjure thee; go with me," and that person would follow, or she herself would change.

What if, in the last moments before Mrs. Tuggle's house had gone up in flames, the old woman had changed herself into a bat—dipped her finger in the cup of tea Mother always kept on her desk and said the conjuring words? Who would have noticed her flying away in all that smoke? And it would explain why only the part of her that was glass—her eye—remained behind, and why there were no bones found at all.

"Come in, please."

The bear himself—Mr. Beasley, in a brown

sweater—opened the door and ushered the small group into his house. There was Lynn, Judith, their father, Mouse, and Dr. Long—the psychologist from elementary school.

When Lynn had told her father everything that had been happening lately, including the rabbit on the front porch and the sound of a voice singing, he said it was time for a conference with Dr. Long—all of them together. And for the first time, they did not all sit around in a circle and stare at Lynn as though she were crazy.

Lynn had told Mother she was going to the Y— that Father was driving her there, going on to the library, and would pick her up later. Judith said she was going to a friend's. And Mother, home by herself with Stevie, did not know about the meeting at the Beasleys', or that the school psychologist would be present. Lynn knew that none of them—she nor Judith nor her father—liked the feeling of leaving Mother out. But neither were they comfortable telling her things that might stir up old feelings in her—feelings that might be related somehow to witchcraft.

Nobody smiled as they seated themselves at the heavy round table in the Beasleys' small dining room. The table seemed to take up most of the room, probably because the walls on all sides of both living and dining rooms and even the hallway were lined with books. All in need of a good dusting. Maybe that was why Mrs. Beasley had left, Lynn thought; she didn't like dusting those books.

Lynn and Mouse sat together at one end of the

table, the school psychologist next to them. Dr. Long spoke in a calm, soft voice.

"Richard here," he told the group, referring to Mr. Morley, "suggested we all meet together and talk about some of the things that have been happening lately. It's obviously time to be concerned. Lynn, tell us what you told your dad."

Lynn did.

"Anyone else have something to tell us? We really don't know what we're dealing with here. We need everybody's thoughts on this."

There was silence around the table.

"Well, I'll start," Dr. Long said. "In August, I took the weed Lynn had given me—that purple flower that was growing along the creek—to a horticulture laboratory at the university to find out what it was. The scientist there confirmed that it was a type of plant called witch weed that he had not seen before, and he planned some tests on it the following day. But when he came to work the next morning, the weed had self-destructed. It had completely crumbled into a fine powder. He had no explanation for this. And because I didn't want to go into all that has been happening here, I didn't tell him any more. I guess, like the rest of you, I was hoping that after Lynn burned the witch weed, this whole business would blow over."

"I'm in somewhat the same situation," Mr. Beasley said. There was a clutter of ceramic mugs on the table amid magazines and a few books. Mr. Beasley had placed a pot of coffee among the cups, but nobody seemed to be drinking. "In the past, I've believed some, but not all, of what Marjorie told me. I believed the strange gathering of cats and crows outside our house one night when I wasn't here, for example, because when I came home, the ground was literally covered with hair and feathers, and a crow had been trapped in our fireplace. But all the rest . . . I just don't know.''

Lynn waited. Mouse waited.

"Something recent has bothered me, though,'' Marjorie's father went on. "Greta Gullone came into my shop the other day.''

Lynn stared.

"She asked if I had any old books on folk medicine. I did have a few, but I could tell they weren't what she was looking for. She finally said she had once seen a book on spells and potions, and wondered if I had anything like that. I said I had, at one time, but had sold it.''

He looked at Dr. Long. "Perhaps I told you that when some girls from Marjorie's school seemed a little too interested in that book this past summer, I became uneasy. I asked Richard to buy it from me for a dollar, just so I could honestly say it had been sold. When all this business is over, he'll sell it back to me for the same amount.''

"And where is the book now?'' Dr. Long asked.

"Under Mom and Dad's bed,'' Lynn answered. "I found it when I was dusting.''

Lynn's father smiled. "If there's a secret to be found, Lynn will find it.''

"In any case,'' Mr. Beasley continued, "Mrs. Gullone asked who had bought the book. I explained that I never reveal the purchases of my customers, but that I might possibly be able to locate another copy for her, though it would cost a great deal, as there are only a few remaining in the world. I was quite surprised when she asked if I would do so, that she would pay any price. I haven't started a book search for it because this worries me. And I'll confess that if I had not known that Elnora died in the fire, I would have sworn that Greta was Mrs. Tuggle herself."

"How could Mrs. Gullone know about your having *Spells and Potions* if she isn't Mrs. Tuggle herself?"

The voice was Lynn's, sailing soft and clear out over the table. She tried not to look at her father, because she didn't want his look to stop her.

"What are you trying to say, Lynn?" asked Dr. Long.

"I'm saying that Mrs. Gullone looks and acts and talks and walks like Mrs. Tuggle. She has a gold tooth where Mrs. Tuggle had one, has one gray eye and one green, just like Mrs. Tuggle, and she knows something that only Mrs. Tuggle would have known."

"Wait a minute," said her father. "Since they're sisters, they could look and act and talk like each other. That's not too surprising."

"But how would she know about the book?" Judith asked.

"They probably wrote to each other. It's quite possible that Elnora Tuggle, before she died, mentioned *Spells and Potions* to her sister."

That was true also. Lynn wondered if her case was crumbling before her eyes.

"But Dad," Judith went on, "don't you think it's a little strange that of all the things two sisters might write to each other about—one in the United States and the other in England—they would write about a book on witchcraft? Unless they were both very, very interested in it, of course. And that's what's bothering us."

Mr. Morley rested his elbows on the table. "Okay, as long as we're all speaking freely, what troubles me most is that if it is witchcraft we've got here, then we're dealing with something that, as far as I know, we've never faced before in this town. I haven't the slightest idea how we try to fight it. And if it's *not* witchcraft, if there's a logical explanation behind everything that's happened, however strange, then we're falsely accusing an old woman just because she's a bit peculiar. We have to be *very* careful not to repeat the witch-hunts. It doesn't take much at all to create mass hysteria, and that's why I don't want a word of what we've talked about to go beyond this room. At least for now. Do we all agree on that?"

"But Dad, she's got all the signs!" Lynn said.

"What signs?"

"The way she stares right through you, her finger-nails like claws, the—"

"That's exactly the kind of thing I'm talking about, Lynn. Do you realize how many people were burned or hanged as witches in the past just because they looked strange, acted a little different,

matched the list that somebody else had made up
about what a witch was supposed to be? We *can't* let
that happen here!" He looked earnestly at Lynn.
"You can understand that, can't you?"

"Yes." Lynn could. She had had doubts from time
to time herself.

"Marjorie?" Mr. Morley turned to Mouse, wanting to be sure he had her agreement too. Everyone
looked down the table at Mouse, who had not said
anything yet.

"There have been other things that weren't just
strange," Mouse said in her small, squeaky voice.
"Things that have not only been peculiar, but impossible to explain. The way the crows followed us
around. The singing, the whispers, the voices which
we did *not* imagine."

Mr. Beasley shook his head. "I can't explain them
either. I simply don't know. Marjorie has an active
imagination, but not *that* wild."

"What concerns me lately is that my wife has
already paid a visit to Mrs. Gullone's, and the
woman herself asked Lynn and Marjorie to help
carry something up to her house, then invited them
in," Lynn's father continued. "If Mrs. Gullone
is . . ." He hesitated, then said it finally, ". . . a witch
. . . and has powers we can't explain, I fear for my
family. We haven't said much to Stevie at all about
this. He's so young. But if even my wife and daugh-
ters are vulnerable . . . *I'm* vulnerable . . . then . . .
Well, what would you suggest, Dr. Long?"

The psychologist sat with his chin in his hands
and thought for some time before answering. "It

might help—in order to be more scientific about this—if we examine what our thoughts and moods were just before something happened. If you hear singing, for example, girls, and there is no explanation where it's coming from, try to think what you were doing or feeling before it began and write it down as honestly as you can. This will at least help us determine *when* the singing occurs. Were you already feeling frightened? Or were you thinking of something else entirely when the singing or the whispers started? We have to examine every angle, be as open as possible, whether we want to accept the possibility or not."

"I don't think that's enough." It was Mr. Beasley now. "I don't see how we can just sit around waiting for Mrs. Gullone to make the first move. That first move could be catastrophic. I think it's time to take action, but who would believe us? If we told the police about the singing, they'd say, 'So who's afraid of a song?' "

Mr. Morley nodded. "That's right. So far, we can't say she's hurt anyone. We have no proof that she's done anything illegal. But one woman in town is dead, probably because of witchcraft. Bertha Voight's case is closed because Mrs. Tuggle is supposedly dead. But if Mrs. Gullone is also involved in witchcraft, do we really want to wait until someone else is murdered? I certainly don't."

Lynn watched her father, Marjorie's father, the school psychologist—their faces tense. Each stared at the table or the wall. Mr. Morley sat rubbing his forehead. At last it was Dr. Long who spoke.

"There's something I could try." Everyone turned. "It's so . . . well . . . far-out that I couldn't bring myself to discuss it with a colleague. But I was looking through some old journals lately for an article I read several years ago, in which it described the treatment for a woman who considered herself a witch. She had indeed done some disturbing things in the neighborhood, though none of them seemed supernatural in any way. She was forced to listen to the complaints against her, and whenever she tried to justify her actions, the psychologists and social worker repeated her own words back to her, over and over again."

"And you think . . . ?" Mr. Beasley paused.

"I've been giving this a lot of thought. I was wondering what would happen if you, Ed, invited Mrs. Gullone over here on a specific evening. Tell her that you have some people who are interested in meeting her, and you thought she might like to get better acquainted in the neighborhood. If she agrees, Richard and I will be here, and once she's inside, we'll confront her with all we know about her and her sister. We'll chant back to her the songs you keep hearing—you girls will have to write down the words for us—and we'll immerse her, so to speak, in her own spells and chants and see what happens."

"And if she gets up to leave?" Mr. Beasley asked.

"We lock the doors," said Dr. Long.

Lynn and Mouse stared at each other uncertainly.

"We're talking lawsuit here," said Lynn's father. "Kidnapping, for starters."

"It's a chance we'll have to take. If she goes to the

police, we tell them why. She would know that we would. Meanwhile, we wouldn't lay a hand on her. Talk only. I'll tell you frankly I haven't the slightest notion whether this would help. They use this confrontational therapy with some success with alcoholics, but whether it would work here. . . ."

"This is a far cry from alcoholics."

"I know. But if nothing else, the fact that three adults, rather than the girls, are confronting her with what they know may at least give her second thoughts, force her to keep the witchcraft in check, if not give it up entirely."

Mr. Beasley looked over at Lynn's father. "I'm willing to give it a try. What about tomorrow night?"

Lynn's father nodded. Dr. Long nodded.

"Where . . . where will *I* be?" Mouse asked, her eyes huge.

"Not here, that's for sure," said her father. "I want you over at Lynn's. I don't want you girls to leave the house, not even once, while this is going on." He turned back to the others. "Mrs. Gullone doesn't have a telephone, Mouse tells me, so I'll stop over there tomorrow on my way to work and issue the invitation. If you don't hear from me, it's on for seven o'clock."

Dr. Long rode home in his own car, but the Morleys rode home together. Judith got out at the corner to go to a girlfriend's house, but when Lynn and her father reached their driveway, Lynn suddenly leaned over and gave him a hug.

"Oh, Dad . . ."

"It's okay, honey," said her father. "We're taking over now. You let us handle it."

Once inside the door, Lynn stopped and sniffed. Something smelled different—like an old woman's rose water cologne or something. She walked over to the doorway of the living room and looked around. There were two teacups on the coffee table, and a plate with crumbs. One last black walnut cookie sat in the middle. But Mother and Stevie were gone.

chapter nine

Lynn stared at the plate, then at her father. "Mrs. Gullone has been here."

"How do you know, Lynn?"

"This is a black walnut cookie."

"So?"

"Dad, she was *here*! She made this! There are two cups on the coffee table. . . ."

"Sylvia!" her father called, going to the foot of the stairs. And then, after a pause, "Stevie?"

No answer. Father went upstairs to check, and when he came back down he said, "I'm going to Mrs. Gullone's. Come with me. I don't want you here by yourself."

Dark clouds rushed over the moon as Lynn and her father went down the steps. It was as though they had left the door to the chicken coop open, let the fox inside. How did Mrs. Gullone know that Mother and Stevie were home by themselves? Had she been watching the house, or what?

When they reached the sidewalk by the curb, dimly lit by streetlamps, and started up the hill, there was still no sign of Stevie or Mother up ahead. Lynn felt that familiar grip of panic. *Disappeared without a trace.* How often had she seen that phrase. . . .

They reached the grove of trees, and then saw the dim light at Mrs. Gullone's front door, shining through the branches of the thorn apple. And coming down the narrow sidewalk from the house were Mother and Stevie.

Lynn and her father stopped.

"Sylvia, we were worried," Father said.

"Why?"

"We got home, there's no sign of you or Stevie. . . . Two cups left on the coffee table, so we knew you had a visitor."

"Only Mrs. Gullone," Mother said. "We walked her home."

"Know what?" Stevie said excitedly. "She's going to let me feed her big rabbit sometime. You want to come, Lynn?"

"I don't think so."

They walked the rest of the way home in silence, broken only by Stevie's chatter.

Once inside the house, Mother and Father went to the kitchen, and Lynn could hear an argument beginning.

"Well, what was I supposed to do, Richard? Tell the old woman she couldn't come in?" Mother was saying, her voice angry, loud.

"I'm more concerned about you and Stevie walking her home in the dark."

"Good heavens, Richard. Just up the street and back . . . !"

"Come on, Stevie, I'll read you your bedtime story," Lynn said, leading the way to the stairs. "Which do you want—*The Biggest Bear* or *I'll Fix Anthony*?"

"Do we have any books about rabbits?" Stevie asked.

"No," said Lynn. "We're reading *The Biggest Bear.*"

Sitting on Stevie's bed, back to the wall, a blanket thrown over their legs, Lynn read him the book. But she realized that her mouth was merely forming the words; none of them registered in her brain.

The way Stevie leaned against her, his head heavy under her arm, one hand resting palm up on her thigh . . . When she glanced down she saw his mouth slightly open, so intent was he on the story. She loved the pinkness of his cheeks, the baby fat that puffed his face out at the sides. He seemed so small and quiet, so unbearably trusting.

It would take so little to lure him up the hill—a song, a sweet, a story, a rabbit. If she ever came home to find him gone, turned perhaps into something the family wouldn't even recognize, would walk right by . . . She leaned over suddenly and hugged him with both arms.

Stevie struggled free. "You weren't done yet, Lynn! You didn't read the last page!"

"I didn't?"

"No. Finish it!"

"I love you, Stevie," she told him instead.

"So finish it!" he insisted, grinning a little.

Lynn did.

"Don't you like bear stories?" Stevie asked when she was done. "Are you scared of bears?"

"Not bears," she said.

"Tigers?"

Lynn was smiling. "Not even tigers," she spoofed.
"Elephants?"
"Nope."
"Rabbits?"
Lynn stopped smiling. "Sometimes," she said.

As she lay in her own bed that night, Lynn wished that Judith had come home with them so they could talk. It always worried her when her parents argued. Perhaps it was because they didn't quarrel that much, so every time they did, it seemed scary. She had known girls at school who said their parents quarreled all the time. Fought, even. She wondered how much the Beasleys had quarreled before they separated.

"Mouse," she said the next day on the bus to junior high. "Tell me something. Did your parents quarrel a lot right before they separated?"

"Uh-uh." Mouse had brought her breakfast with her, and held it in her lap. There was a fried-egg sandwich and an orange.

"They didn't?"

"They hardly quarreled at all. Mostly they didn't say anything to each other. It was sort of like, 'Marjorie, go ask your mother if she paid the electric bill this month,' or 'Marjorie, please tell your father his dinner's on the stove.' Stuff like that. I began to feel like Western Union."

Lynn felt even worse. She tried to concentrate on the day ahead. The evening, in particular.

"As soon as we get home from school, I'll tell Mom I've invited you to dinner. Come early," she said.

"Do you think it will work, Lynn? What our dads are planning?"

Lynn sucked in her breath. "I don't know," she said, "and neither do they."

Lynn could think of little else all day. The scary part about last night was what Mrs. Gullone was after—why she had come when nobody was home except Mom and Stevie. So when Lynn got back from school that afternoon, she decided to ask, and had the perfect opportunity when she saw some little cakes on a plate on the table.

"Where'd we get those?" she asked, picking one up, suspecting.

"Mrs. Gullone brought them along with the cookies when she came yesterday. Wasn't that thoughtful of her?"

Lynn wondered whether or not she should eat it.

"Have you tasted one yet?" she asked.

"Yes, and they're delicious."

Mother had eaten one and was still alive. Lynn closed her eyes and bit into it, wondering what to say next. She would have more luck keeping Mother talking if she tried to keep things casual.

"Why did she bring *us* stuff? She's the new neighbor."

Mother was peeling apples to make applesauce. "It's sort of an old custom, you know. When someone brings you food, it's polite to return the dishes with something in them. These are tea cakes, I think—scones, she called them."

"So is she settled in?"

"Yes, I think so. I guess she's lonely here, though. Just seemed to want to talk."

Lynn remembered Mouse. "Mouse is lonely, too, and I invited her to dinner tonight. Okay?"

"Of course."

Lynn took another bite, chewed and swallowed, watching the curl of apple peeling in her mother's hands get longer and longer. "What did you talk about, you and Mrs. Gullone? England?"

"Oh, this and that. I told her she was the very image of her sister, and she said everybody always did mix them up."

"What else did she say?"

"Well, she loves to read, and wanted to know if we had any good books she could borrow. I told her to browse through the bookshelves and she could borrow anything that looked interesting. I don't believe she took any, though."

Lynn discreetly put the rest of her tea cake back on the table. "Anything else?"

Mrs. Morley was measuring water into the big kettle on the stove. "You're the curious one now, aren't you! Let's see . . . she saw that I was making applesauce, and said she'd like to start a little club for neighborhood girls."

Lynn stared. "What *kind* of club?"

"A cooking club, I guess. I'm not sure. Maybe she's thinking about teaching girls to make tea scones."

Lynn went up to her room and dumped her books on the bed. She took her journal out from under the mattress and wrote, in big letters, *IT'S HER AGAIN,*

I KNOW IT! Mrs. Tuggle, or Mrs. Gullone, is trying to form a coven, and Mother's falling for it, just as she did before.

"Judith," she said, when her sister came home. "What are we going to do?" Lynn told her everything.

"*We're* not going up to Mrs. Gullone's to take cooking lessons, that's for sure. And if we find out that anyone else is, we'll stop them," Judith replied, and sat down.

"Judith, I'm scared."

"So am I. Let's be sure to tell Dad about this before they confront her tonight. That's another thing they should know."

Lynn called Mouse next to warn her, just in case.

"Mouse, did you ever want to learn to make tea cakes?"

"I don't know. Are they chocolate?"

"Any kind at all."

"Maybe. Are they any good?"

"Mouse, listen! The point is you shouldn't. I mean, Mrs. Gullone is trying to start a cooking class, we think, for girls in the neighborhood, but I know it's just an excuse to start a witches' coven."

"Oh, Lordy! Is dinner ready yet, Lynn?"

"Not quite."

"I'm coming over anyway."

Lynn and Mouse sat on the window seat in the music room, hugging their knees. Stevie was crawling around in the hallway, running his Matchbox cars along the baseboard and humming to himself.

"Lynn," Mother called from the kitchen. "Your father just phoned and said he'd like an early dinner. He has a meeting at seven. Set the table, please."

The girls jumped up and joined Judith in the dining room. They exchanged knowing looks.

But Mr. Morley never did make it home to eat. He phoned again to say he was sorry, but some work at the office had detained him. He'd get a sandwich somewhere and go directly to the meeting. Lynn lost her chance to tell him about the cooking club.

Thinking about it later, she could scarcely remember what they had eaten for dinner or who had said what. Her eyes seemed to be on the clock in the living room. Now Mrs. Gullone was probably finishing her supper; now she was rinsing her dishes; now she was putting on her coat; now she was starting down the hill toward the Beasleys'. . . .

At ten to seven, Lynn, Mouse, and Judith were sitting on the edge of Judith's bed on the third floor, and Lynn was not sure she could stand the suspense. As frightened as she was when she was around Mrs. Gullone, this was even worse—not knowing. From downstairs came the sound of running water for Stevie's bath, Mother's voice in the hallway, Stevie's complaints.

Five to seven.

"Do you think she's there yet?" Mouse breathed, eyes on Judith's clock.

"Probably just turning the corner," Lynn said. "Oh, she's going to be furious when she gets there and finds out what it's all about."

"Dad didn't lie," Mouse said. "They *are* people who want to meet her."

"But it's no friendly neighborhood gathering," Judith added.

"How long do you think it will take? Dr. Long was talking about five hours."

"Mom will start to get worried. She'll wonder where Dad is, why he's not coming home, why Mouse is staying here," Judith said.

Bong, bong, bong. . . . The grandfather clock in the downstairs hall began to chime the hour.

Lynn looked toward the window. She was sure that the last time she'd looked, she had seen gray sky. Now, in the space of a few minutes—seconds, even—it was entirely black.

"Listen!"

At first Lynn thought it was a hiss, a whisper, even. Then she realized it was a whistle, and at last she knew what it was. The wind. A sudden wind had come up, whistling through the cracks around the windows. Doors rattled. A shutter flapped.

"Gracious!" came Mother's voice from a floor down. "What a wind!"

For a moment the lights flickered, grew dim, then brightened again.

Mouse sat without moving, but Lynn went to the window and looked out. She could see nothing at all. No clouds, no sky, not even a hint of moon.

And then, as suddenly as the wind had started, it stopped.

There was the sound of water running out of the

bathtub, Stevie's feet thudding across the hall. The squeak of his bedsprings, Mother's voice, reading a bedtime story.

At seven forty-five, Mr. Beasley came for Mouse.

At eight o'clock, Dad came home. Lynn and Judith waited on Judith's bed as they heard him talking to Mother.

"That was a short meeting," Mother said.

"Over sooner than I expected," he answered, and came on upstairs.

With a sinking feeling, Lynn faced her father as he entered the room. He shook his head. "She didn't show," he said softly. "At seven sharp, there was a rap on the door, Ed answered, and a gust of wind blew in. But she wasn't there, and never came. Ed drove up to her house to see if she needed a ride, but she never answered the door."

She knows! Lynn thought.

"What are we going to do, Dad?" Judith asked.

"We haven't decided yet," he said. "But it's our problem, not yours. Don't worry."

That was something Lynn couldn't do. If there was a way not to worry, she didn't know how.

"She knows!" she told Judith after her father had gone downstairs.

"Of course she does. She seems to know everything before it happens." Judith stood up and stared at her own reflection in the mirror. "I wish we could leave here! Just go to California or somewhere and start a new life!"

"You know we can't."

"I know Dad won't. Can't and won't are two different things."

"He'd say we were running away from the problem."

"I'd say fine. Has he got a better solution? No."

It was Stevie and Mother whom Lynn worried about most. Long after the lights were out, she wondered what she could say to Mother to help her understand that Mrs. Gullone was dangerous. What she could say to Stevie to keep him away from the house on the hill without making him suspicious of *all* new neighbors or *all* elderly women.

Somewhere, she thought, in *Spells and Potions*, she had read about a charm for children that would protect them from witchcraft. She tried to remember what it was. A verse? A trinket? The only thing that came to mind were the words

Wind and water, earth and sky,
Keep me safe from witches.

She'd need something more for Stevie—innocent little Stevie—who would not only walk an old lady home, but go inside her house if she asked him. And it was simply a matter of time before she asked.

"Mouse," she said the next day. "I'm afraid for Stevie. I'm afraid Mrs. Gullone has her eye on him next."

"For cooking school?"

"For anything."

"Just don't let her dip him or any part of him in

milk or water," Mouse said as their bus pulled up to the school. "If the book is right, and if that *is* part of what it takes for a witch to bodily transfigure somebody, you could come home some day and find Stevie turned into a hamster."

"Don't joke." The girls got off and went inside the building.

"I'm sorry," Mouse said. "But check that book. It seems there *was* something—a charm, maybe, for small children to wear on their clothes."

"I wish . . ." Lynn began wistfully. "I wish we could get a piece of consecrated chalk to draw around everybody we love to protect them."

"That would be sort of selfish, though," Mouse said as they reached their lockers. "Just people we love? You want to draw a circle around everybody in Indiana—protect them all from Mrs. Gullone?"

"It would be easier to draw a circle around Mrs. Gullone and keep the evil *in*," Lynn declared, and decided she would check the book when she got home to see if that were possible.

When she reached her house that afternoon and started up the walk, she saw Stevie on his knees in the side yard, sitting motionless.

Lynn came around the house to see what he was doing, and he turned, one finger to his lips.

"Shhh," he said. "The rabbit."

Lynn put her books on the ground and crouched down beside him. Near the weeds along the fence, the large gray rabbit sat not ten feet away, but its

big dark eye watched Stevie and Lynn. It was up on its haunches, front paws dangling.

"It's Mrs. Gullone's rabbit," Stevie said, "but I'm going to learn to feed it. Its name is Delcy."

"How do you know?" Lynn whispered back.

"It told me."

"Told you its name?"

"I said, 'Hi, Rabbit. What's your name?' and it said, 'Delcy.' "

A great uneasiness swept over Lynn. "Stevie, are you just making that up, or did the rabbit really talk?"

"It *talked*, Lynn! It said, 'Del-cy,' just like that."

The rabbit hopped off into the bushes, and Lynn decided not to say anymore about it. "Where's Mom?" she asked.

"Writing, I think. In the dining room."

Lynn took her books inside and stole quietly upstairs to the second floor. She tiptoed into her parents' bedroom, knelt down by the bed, and stretched out one arm. Lynn felt only the headboard against the wall. Her fingers touched nothing else. She thrust her arm as far under as it would reach, sweeping it back and forth. Nothing but bare floor.

Lynn put her cheek against the floor and looked. The space beneath her parents' bed was empty. The sack with *Spells and Potions* in it was gone.

"Looking for something, Lynn?"

The voice came from behind her. Lynn whirled around and sat up.

Mother stood unsmiling there in the doorway.

chapter ten

"Mother!" Lynn scrambled to her feet. "Stevie said that you were still writing . . . and I didn't want to bother you. . . ."

There was something about Mother's voice, her face, her eyes, that made Lynn's knees feel shaky.

"So you came in here? You lost something, perhaps?"

Lynn's knees shook all the harder.

"If you were looking for *Spells and Potions*, Lynn, I have it," Mrs. Morley said, and, turning, went back downstairs.

Lynn stood for a moment, speechless, her heart pounding wildly, then fled up to her room. She was still sitting there, in the same position, her jacket on, when Judith walked in ten minutes later.

"Lynn, what's the matter? You look like you've seen a ghost!"

Lynn pulled her sister down beside her. "Mother has the book," she said hoarsely.

Judith's mouth dropped. "She found it?"

Lynn nodded. "I was going to look up charms to protect Stevie. I reached under the bed, and the book was gone. Mom came in and asked what I was doing."

"Oh, my gosh! What did you say?"

"What could I say? Then she said, 'If you're look-ing for *Spells and Potions*, I have it.' And left. She was so *strange*, Judith!"

Judith swallowed, her face pale. "Oh, Lynn!" She looked about quickly. "Where's Stevie?"

"Outside."

"Let's keep him up here with us until Dad gets home."

"Do ... do you think that ... Mother ... ?"

"I don't know what to think. Let's just get Stevie."

Lynn went back downstairs, holding on to the railing lest her legs buckle beneath her. The house was quiet. She didn't know where Mother was and didn't try to find out. She went directly outside and found Stevie at the back of the garden. He was holding out a piece of grass and the large gray rabbit was closer now, only a few feet away from his hand.

Stevie grinned when he saw her. "See, Lynn?" he whispered. "I'm *taming* him."

"Come inside, Stevie," Lynn said in response, lift-ing him up by one arm. "It's getting cold out here. Judith and I want you to come up to our room. We're going to play a game or something."

"Don't be afraid of a *rabbit*, Lynn! He's nice!"

"I'm not afraid. I just think you ought to come in." She gave him a tug.

They turned and started toward the house, and then a voice said behind them, "Del-cy."

Lynn whirled around, but no one was there. Only the rabbit.

"See?" Stevie said. "That's his name, all right."

Lynn rushed Stevie into the house and up to her room.

It was a strange supper. Lynn and Judith came to the table with Stevie. There were potatoes, some pork chops and a salad, some sliced peaches and the rest of Mrs. Gullone's tea cakes for dessert, but Mother was quiet.

Lynn tried to avoid her mother's eyes, but each time she looked up, Mother seemed to be looking right at her. Looking *through* her, even. Lynn put her fork down, feeling sick. Scared. Judith was trying to carry on a conversation with Stevie about what he had done at school, trying to make the evening seem normal, but even she was having a rough time of it. If only Dad would come.

Mrs. Morley said nothing at all. Not even "Don't kick the table, Stevie" or "Please pass the potatoes." She sat and stared, stared and sat, and whenever Lynn lifted her knife or fork, there were Mother's eyes, looking through her.

The phone rang in the hallway and Lynn almost knocked over her chair in her rush to answer it, to leave the table. If it was Dad, she'd tell him to come home immediately, that something was wrong with Mom. It was Mouse.

"L-Lynn, come over!"

"Why? What's wrong?"

"I'm scared!"

"Why?"

"I don't know. Hurry."

Lynn started to tell Marjorie to come over to her house instead, but not knowing what was going on with Mother, thought better of it.

She went back to the dinner table. "Mouse wants me to come over," she said. "It's important." She was looking at Judith as she said it.

For a moment they tried to read each other's minds. Did she dare go and leave Stevie and Judith here alone with Mother? Did she dare *not* go and find out what was happening at the Beasleys'?

"Go on," said Judith. "Dad will be here soon."

"What difference does that make?" Mother asked, the strange look in her eyes.

"See you," Lynn said in answer, which was no answer at all, and, grabbing her jacket, ran outside and down the street.

Halfway to Marjorie's, the corners of Lynn's mouth sagged as though she were about to cry. She was both sad and terrified, and knew she should not be going to Mouse's alone. Where was Mr. Beasley? Surely not at home, or Mouse wouldn't have had to call. Lynn knew she should have called Dad at his office, but chances were he was on his way home. She should have called Dr. Long, then. But by then she was halfway down the hill, so she went on, turned onto a side street, and a few minutes later ran up the steps of the Beasley home.

Mouse answered her knock and pulled her inside. "Stay with me, Lynn, till Dad gets here."

"What's *happened*?"

"Nothing yet. I just have the feeling someone's out there."

"Great! Why didn't you *tell* me?"

"Because I couldn't see anyone. It's just this weird feeling."

"Why didn't you call your dad?"

"I did, but he's not at the store. I think he had an auction to go to."

"Well, I'm scared, too. Things are getting really creepy at home. Oh, Mouse! I went upstairs to get *Spells and Potions* and it wasn't there! Mom walked in and saw me, and said that *she* has it, and she looked so strange. She *sounds* strange. Judith told me to bring Stevie up to our room and keep him with us till Dad gets home, and when I went to bring him in, he was with Mrs. Gullone's gray rabbit. He said he asked the rabbit its name and it spoke to him. Said its name was Delcy. I think I heard it, too, as I was bringing Stevie in."

Mouse slumped down in a chair. "Everything's beginning again, I know it! Lynn, don't leave."

"I'll stay."

"Let's have dinner together."

"I just ate."

"Well, eat again."

Knock, knock, knock.

"L-Lordy!"

There was a light, sharp rap at the door, almost like a bird pecking with its beak.

"L-Lynn . . . !"

"I'll go with you."

Together the girls went back through the dark hallway to the front door.

"Don't open it until you look, Mouse."

Marjorie was already peering out a small window at one side of the door.

"There's someone there, but I can't make out who it is."

The tapping came again, more urgent, commanding the girls, it seemed, to open the door.

Mouse turned the handle. Immediately the door swung open and Mrs. Gullone was inside.

It happened so quickly that Lynn could scarcely think. Her first impulse was to shove the woman back out again, but she could not imagine herself doing such a thing. And before either girl could think what to do, Mrs. Gullone groped her way to a chair just inside the living room, one hand on her chest.

"Glad I am that you were home, dearie, because I feel a faintness," she said to Mouse. "Out for my nightly walk, and this old body's not as strong as it used to be."

Marjorie stood pressed against the wall as though someone had pasted her to it. Lynn knew she had to take over.

"If you're sick, Mrs. Gullone, I'll call an ambulance," she said.

"Oh, no no," the woman said quickly, reaching out to grab Lynn's arm. Her nails, like the claws of a chicken, made an odd scratch on the skin. "A drink of water and a little rest, and I'll be on my way."

"I'll stay here with her," Lynn told Mouse, determined not to let Mrs. Gullone out of their sight. "You get the water, and when she's rested, we'll help her down the steps."

Mouse came unglued from the wall and walked mechanically back to the kitchen. Mrs. Gullone had her eyes on Lynn all the while.

"What were you doing walking way down here?" Lynn asked, trying to keep her voice polite. Trying, in fact, to keep it from shaking. "It's dark outside, and the hill's steep."

"Why, Lynn girl, on the Isle of Man I walked for miles light or dark, fair or rain, uphill or down, it made no difference. It does an old woman no good, you know, to sit around and grow stiff."

Lynn would not allow herself to be fooled. "Why did you come down to the Beasleys'?" she asked.

Mrs. Gullone's eyes became slits as she focused hard on Lynn. "A rude tongue you have in your mouth, dearie."

Lynn stood her ground. "I won't let you hurt Mouse."

"Why should I hurt her? What would put an idea like that in your head?"

Marjorie came back from the kitchen and handed a glass of water to Mrs. Gullone.

"You're kind to this old woman," the lady crooned, fastening her eyes on Marjorie this time. "Ah! A few minutes more and these bones will be able to go on."

For the first time since she'd arrived, Mrs. Gullone's eyes left the girls and surveyed the room around her. Her head turned slowly as though her eyes were a movie camera. "There used to be a salve—a potion—my mother told me about, that would help aches such as mine. 'Twas in an old book, I think, *Spells and Potions*, and if I could find it, it would heal my aches, and I could walk ten miles, I'll wager. The salve would keep me fit."

Lynn could find no words to answer. Marjorie's eyes were huge as she stared first at the old woman, then at Lynn. But Mrs. Gullone went on scanning the bookshelves—the living room, the dining room, the hall. . . . "Would that book be here, do you think, Marjorie girl?"

"Mouse!" Lynn cautioned, then wished she hadn't, for the old woman attached her eyes to Lynn again.

"Eh?" she said, and her lips began to smile. "Some secret the child isn't telling me? You would keep such a book for yourselves when it might help an old woman get about?"

"It's time for you to go, Mrs. Gullone," Lynn told her. "Would you like some help going down the front steps?" Lynn could scarcely believe the words that were coming from her own mouth.

In answer, Mrs. Gullone closed her eyes as though she were suddenly seized with another pain. "All mixed up," she mumbled. "My head . . . this old head . . . all confused. Things are all sixes and sevens, sixes and sevens. Sevens . . . sevens . . ." she continued, her eyes still closed, and suddenly they were open again, looking straight at Marjorie as she chanted: "Sevens . . . sevens . . . Sevena . . . Sevena . . ."

Marjorie's other name! The name Mrs. Tuggle had called her once to force her out of the chalk circle in the cellar of the old house.

"Where is the book, Sevena?" Mrs. Gullone continued in her chanting, singsong voice.

"S-someone's got it," Marjorie stammered, her own eyes drowsy.

"Mouse!" Lynn cried.

"Who?" Mrs. Gullone was leaning forward, her eyes riveted on Mouse. "Who has the book, Sevena? Tell me, Sevena, tell me!"

"Stop it!" Lynn yelled, and suddenly jumped to one side as she saw Mrs. Gullone's hand move. A moment later the water in the old woman's glass splashed beside her on the floor.

Mrs. Gullone's eyes were harder still. Small and narrow, hard and cold.

"Marjorie!" Lynn commanded. "Go bring the salt." It had withered the witch weed once. Maybe it could do the same to a witch.

At the sound of Lynn's voice calling her "Marjorie," Mouse blinked and stared at the water on the floor, then at Mrs. Gullone, whose wrinkled hand, holding the empty glass, trembled in fury. Mouse turned suddenly and headed for the kitchen once again, and as she did, Mrs. Gullone got to her feet.

"Take care, Lynn girl, for I am far, far older than you and a great deal wiser," she said, setting the glass on the lamp table.

And then, needing no help whatsoever, she turned and walked swiftly from the room, opened the front door herself, and disappeared into the night.

Lynn locked the door behind her, then sat down

on the deacon's bench in the hallway, pulse racing. Mouse came out of the kitchen carrying the salt, then stared at the empty chair where the old lady had been.

"Is she gone?"

Lynn nodded weakly. "For now."

"She . . . she called me Sevena."

"I know."

Mouse sat down on the bench beside Lynn, and wiped her eyes, crying silently.

"That name," Mouse wept. "It controls everything that's awful inside me, Lynn. I'm terrified of what I might do."

"That's half its power. We're so afraid it will *make* us do something that this almost comes true. But we were so *stupid*, Mouse, to let her in! We never should have opened the door."

"She knows about the book."

"Of course she does. And all about us and everything."

There was the sound of a car turning into the driveway.

"Dad's home," Mouse said, relieved. She got a tissue and blew her nose. "Oh, Lynn, if you hadn't come, I might not even be here. I'm sure of it. I don't know how I knew she was out there. I just did."

"Tell your dad *everything*, Mouse! He's got to know. He shouldn't leave you here by yourself. Not anymore. Not after tonight."

Mouse jumped up and grabbed Lynn's arm. "Come on. I'm going to ask him to drive you home.

You can help me tell him what happened on the way."

When Lynn got inside her own house, she heard her mother's voice coming from upstairs, bartering with Stevie about how many books he could look at before "lights out." Lynn walked into the living room where Dad and Judith were talking in low voices.

"What was wrong at Marjorie's?" Judith asked, looking up, and Lynn told them about Mrs. Gullone.

"You didn't let her *in*!" Judith gasped.

Lynn tried to explain.

"Lynn, don't *ever*—!" her father began, but Lynn interrupted.

"Dad, you just don't know. It was like . . . oh, I don't know . . . someone tapping, then banging. Mouse put her hand on the doorknob and the next thing we knew, Mrs. Gullone was inside. And I'm sure that she's after the book. I think it's what she wanted when she came here."

"Maybe so, but right now it's your mother I'm worried about," said Mr. Morley. "Judith says *she* has the book. She's been so quiet the past few days, I think it's time we—"

"Time we what, Richard?"

Everyone turned as Mother herself walked into the room.

chapter eleven

The silence in the room was so heavy that Lynn felt she could almost reach out and touch it. Taste it on her tongue. She looked at her father, but he seemed to be having trouble speaking himself.

Finally he said, "We're worried about you, Sylvia."

"And so it's time to what?" Mother repeated. "Lock me up in a room? Allow me no visitors? Make all my decisions for me?"

"Sylvia, please sit down," Father said gently. "*This* is what I meant. That it's time we all had a serious talk together."

"You should have done that a long time ago, Richard." Mother sat down, but tensely on the edge of a chair, not leaning back at all. "These past few months I've watched the rest of you exchange looks when I come in a room, heard you whisper behind my back, and treat me like a fragile Christmas tree ornament that might break if you gave me a jolt."

Lynn huddled beside Judith on the couch, scarcely daring to breathe. There were times lately she felt she had lost touch with her mother completely—hardly knew her at all. Had the experience with Mrs. Tuggle changed her that much?

Would the family ever be back to the way they had been before the old woman affected their lives? Was Lynn, in fact, in a room with a woman who was her mother or a— She couldn't allow herself to think the *W* word, even here.

"We didn't want you to get sick again." Her father's voice. Everyone was watching Mother.

"I wasn't sick. I was confused. I couldn't believe that such a lonely old lady like Mrs. Tuggle could be evil. I didn't think I was so vulnerable that—even if she *were* evil—she could affect me. Yet none of you wanted to talk with me about it. Whenever I brought up the subject, you'd all start discussing something else."

Lynn listened, her lips apart. So all the time, Mother knew! All the time they were trying to protect her, they were really closing her out.

"Sylvia, I'm sorry," Father said. "I just didn't want all that business starting again."

"All *what* business, Richard? Say it. For once in your life, say the word! Witchcraft. Because that's what it is, isn't it? With Mrs. Tuggle? And now Mrs. Gullone?"

"Mom, you *knew* . . . ?" Judith asked in astonishment.

"I've suspected, just like you. Suspected that she had some kind of hold over me in the past. But it won't happen again, Richard, because I'm not going to *let* it happen. I'm not going to let Mrs. Gullone, who*ever* she is, do harm to my family."

"Oh, Mom!" Lynn couldn't help herself. She got up and flung herself into her mother's chair, into her mother's arms, and gave her the hug she had wanted to give for so long. The Mom she had missed was back.

Mother hugged too—hard—the confident kind of squeeze that let Lynn know she meant it, and then Lynn sat down on the floor beside her, her arms wrapped around her Mother's legs, as though, now that Mom was back, Lynn wouldn't let her go.

"But Sylvia, if you've been worried about Mrs. Gullone too, why on earth did you and Stevie walk home with her the other night?"

"I wanted proof that she's up to something. She asked us to walk her home, and I wanted to find out what she would say when we got there, how she would try to lure us in. With the rabbit, of course. That's how she's planning to lure Stevie. I wanted you to talk about it then, but you wouldn't. I gave you every chance, but all you'd say was that we didn't know Mrs. Gullone that well. We know Mrs. Gullone and what she's up to *too* well, Richard."

"Mom, who do you think she is?" Judith asked. "Really."

"I don't know who she is, but I know who she is not. She is *not* Mrs. Tuggle's sister, because Elnora Tuggle didn't have any."

Lynn gasped. She saw her father stare. "How do you *know*, Sylvia?" he asked.

"I checked. I called Castletown on the Isle of Man and asked for the town registrar. They tell me there was a brother registered in the family, but no sisters."

Dad seemed surprised. "You called *England*, Sylvia?"

"I research the books I write, Richard; why not this? I should have learned a little something by now, don't you think?"

Lynn saw a smile exchanged between them, and felt a sudden wild hope that things were somehow going to be all right. Maybe.

"I also asked if a Greta Gullone was registered. There is none at all, married or otherwise."

"Then who *is* she?" asked Father.

"Mrs. Tuggle," said Lynn. And for once, nobody argued.

"But how. . . ?" Father looked confused.

Lynn dared not risk his disbelief by telling him her theory of bodily transfiguration—that Mrs. Tuggle had temporarily transformed herself into a bat to escape the fire, and then turned back into a woman. Or that her brother Clyde had been turned into the large gray rabbit and was acting as her familiar until she decided she needed him more as a boy—a young man, or warlock, for her coven.

"Somehow," Lynn said, "I think she escaped the fire and got away before anyone saw her."

"Unlikely, but possible, I'll admit," Father said.

Judith shook her head. "But it still doesn't explain why she came here in the first place. All the way from England to this little town, just for *Spells and Potions*?"

"Well, not quite," said Mother. "After I found the book under our bed, I put it safely away at the back of my closet, but I've been reading it myself. I've learned that a witch is considered more powerful if she can establish a coven of witches, and that young girls and boys are the easiest to persuade."

"There are young girls and boys in England! There are young people on the Isle of Man! She didn't have to come all the way to the United States," said Father.

Mother went on: "The registrar in Castletown gave me the name of someone who had known Elnora Tuggle as a young girl, and I called her next. 'Elnora?' she said, when I mentioned the name. 'Oh, it was Ellie we called her when she was a girl, a wee thing. Ellie Martin, that was her maiden name.' The woman was very helpful, Richard. She said she used to go over to Ellie Martin's to play with her kitten. But as Elnora grew older, she seemed to change, and eventually got into trouble with some of her neighbors for practicing witchcraft, and was asked to leave. A relative who had immigrated to this country died and left his land here to any surviving relatives, which happened to be Elnora, who was married by then. Her neighbors had been wanting her to go, she had a place to go to, so why not? The people in our town have been surprisingly innocent and unsuspecting, and there were only two main obstacles to forming a coven here: Bertha Voight, who is dead, and *Spells and Potions*, which Lynn and Marjorie discovered in Mr. Beasley's bookstore. A witch does not want her secrets revealed, and she wants that book destroyed. Destroyed, or in her own possession, I'm not sure which."

"According to Mr. Beasley," Judith said, "this copy is one of the few left in the world."

Lynn hugged her mother's legs even harder. "And if that's true, Mom, you're in real danger. We're all in danger, just because the book is here."

"I could put it in a safe-deposit box," Father suggested.

"No. It's valuable to me in predicting what she might try next, or how she'll go about it." Mother looked around the room. "We're going to use it to smoke her out. If she suspects the book is here now, she'll try *some*thing to get it, and I intend to be ready."

"Meaning what?" asked Father. "Surely you're not going to try witchcraft yourself."

"Richard, have a little faith in me for once. I intend to use the law. I'll have her arrested for breaking and entering, or theft, or whatever else I can, and then perhaps the authorities will start an investigation."

"And you really think you can do this alone?"

"I don't have to. I have all of you. We have each other. But I want you girls to promise—*promise*—that you won't let Mrs. Gullone in for any reason whatever."

"We won't," said Judith.

"When she was here the other night—when Stevie and I were alone—she was looking for excuses to take a peek at our bookshelves, and I had a suspicion what she was after." Mother turned her attention to Dad next. "And Richard, I want *you* to

promise that no matter what happens or what you
find out, you'll tell me. No more treating me as if
I were three years old, or so weak and unstable I
can't handle it."

"You have my word. I wish I'd done this long
before."

"So that's what happened, Mouse," Lynn said as the
girls melted chocolate to make fudge the next afternoon. "After Dad went to take his shower, Judith
and I stayed in the living room a long time, talking
to Mom. We told her *every*thing, Mouse—about the
witch weed and the eye, and you know what? I think
she already suspected or guessed most of it. More
than that, I think she believes it."

"Everything?"

"Well, she believes Mrs. Gullone is probably Mrs.
Tuggle. Now there are seven of us to fight Mrs. Gullone or whoever she is."

What Lynn didn't tell Mouse was the way Mother
had hugged and hugged her and Judith, one arm
around each, as though she owed them a lot of lov-
ing. Didn't tell Mouse what a wonderful feeling it
was to know that her mother was *not* practicing
witchcraft, was *not* under Mrs. Gullone's spell, that
she could be trusted, and that there was nothing she
wouldn't do to save her children. Lynn didn't tell
Mouse that because she knew it would only make
Marjorie miss her own mother all the more.

But she didn't have to. Mouse made the connec-
tion herself.

"You know what I'd like?" Mouse said as she thoughtfully stirred in the milk and sugar. "I think I'd like a dog or something. A puppy, maybe. Something that would be waiting for me when I got home from school."

Lynn knew immediately why she brought it up.

"That would be really nice, Mouse," she said. The better things were going in her own family, the sorrier she felt for Mouse. After she and Judith had finally gone to bed the night before, she had come back down to the bathroom later—about one o'clock—and she could hear her parents' voices from their bedroom, talking, talking. Their voices were gentle. It was a wonderful sound.

"How long am I supposed to stir this?" Mouse asked as the chocolatey mixture in the pan began to bubble.

"Don't stir it at all now. We're just supposed to let it simmer until it reaches the soft-ball stage. I promised Stevie I'd let him lick the pan." Lynn went to the kitchen door and opened it. The glider was covered now, and a sharp breeze blew across the porch where they had spent the lazy days of summer. The leaves on the trees in the backyard were already beginning to turn.

"Stevie," she called. "The fudge will be ready to pour in about ten minutes, and then you can lick the pan."

Stevie was traipsing around the backyard looking for caterpillars. "Okay," he said. "Save me the spoon too."

Lynn went back inside the kitchen. "Mom said to watch him all the time when he's out. She won't let him play in the front yard at all. She's afraid Mrs. Gullone will see him there and talk him into going home with her."

"Where is everyone?"

"They went to Sears to get a new dresser for Judith. They'll be back in an hour or so. Want to stay for dinner?"

"Sure."

Mouse wanted to add peanut butter and marshmallow sauce to the fudge after it reached the softball stage, and that made it cool all the faster. As soon as it began to crinkle around the edge of the pan, Lynn poured it into a buttered glass dish. She went to the door again.

"Stevie," she called. "You can lick the pan."

No answer.

She crossed the porch and went out on the steps. "Stevie! Come on. The fudge is ready."

Dry leaves rustled against the eaves of the roof. The sky was growing grayer as evening closed in.

Suddenly, Lynn turned and hurried back inside. "Mouse, Stevie's gone."

Marjorie was setting the glass dish in a pan of cold water to help it cool. She looked up over the tops of her large glasses. "Oh, Lynn! I forgot to tell you! I saw that rabbit on my way over."

"Where?"

"Under some bushes. I was going to tell you, but I got to thinking about fudge and—"

Panic exploded in Lynn's chest. "Get your jacket, Mouse! Hurry! We've got to find him."

Furious at herself for allowing this to happen, and terrified beyond consolation, Lynn stumbled out the front door. She had been asked to watch Stevie, and it had been at least five minutes since she'd looked out the window. A lot could happen in five minutes.

"W-where are we going to look?" Mouse asked as they ran down the front steps.

"Where do you think? There's only one place that the rabbit would take him, if it's her familiar, as I think."

"Your folks don't want you going up there, Lynn."

"What do you suppose they'd say if they knew I let Stevie go up there and didn't go after him?"

Everything about Mrs. Gullone's house seemed to have aged since Lynn saw it last. The thorn apple was bare and scrawny, its branches like claws as the girls passed. There was no light on at all inside, but dry, rustling noises told Lynn that someone was working there in the yard. In the twilight, she could just make out Mrs. Gullone bending over the strangest plants she had ever seen. Then she realized that they were not plants at all, but small saplings that had been uprooted, then turned upside down, their trunks thrust into the soil like spears, their roots, like writhing snakes, stretching outward in all directions.

"Ah!" said the old woman, straightening up when

she saw them. "Come to help an old woman tend her garden?"

"I've come for Stevie," Lynn said.

"Well, my girl, I haven't got him."

"Have you *seen* him, then?" Lynn demanded. "We think he followed the gray rabbit, and if he did, he must have come here."

"Eh? You speak in riddles."

"No, I don't. The rabbit's name is Delcy, Mrs. Gullone, it belongs to you, and Stevie must be here."

"Is it a crime, then, to feed a rabbit, to show a little care?"

"It may be a crime to practice witchcraft, Mrs. Gullone. I want my brother back."

The old woman seemed not to have heard. She bent over the strangely shaped roots again: "My Medusa plants," she said, and her laugh was more like a cackle. "I pull up trees when they're young, you see—wild trees back of my property—and dry them out like this. Then I cut them into tidy pieces and use them for tinder, don't you see?"

The more she talked, the more she seemed to be referring to children—small children—taken when they were young. Lynn began to panic.

"Stevie?" she called out, looking around. "Stevie!"

And then, from around the house, Stevie came skipping, as though he was unaware that he had wandered off and the girls were looking for him.

"Did you see it, Lynn?" he asked. "Did you see

Delcy? I was giving it grass, and it ate right out of my hand."

"You *know* you're not supposed to leave the yard without telling someone," Lynn scolded, relief washing over her. She grabbed his hand, Mouse grabbed the other, and they rushed him down the walk to the street.

But behind them, they heard Mrs. Gullone laugh, and it was only then that Lynn realized that the letters of *Delcy* could be rearranged to spell *Clyde*.

chapter twelve

"Where've you been?" Judith was on the front porch when they came up the steps. "The door was half open, and there's a dish of fudge in the kitchen that's already hard. It was as though a wind had blown in and carried you off."

"Stevie went up to Mrs. Gullone's without asking," Lynn reported. "He *knows* he's not supposed to do that."

Stevie was glaring.

Judith knelt down and grasped him by both shoulders. "Stevie, please! You *mustn't* go up there anymore."

"*Why?* I was just following Delcy. He *wanted* me to come."

The girls looked at Stevie, then at each other.

"Listen!" Judith continued. "We think something is the matter with Mrs. Gullone. With her mind. We're afraid she might try to hurt you."

This time Stevie stared back. "She's *nice!*"

"We just don't know that. Not for sure. And you *must* not go up there, Stevie. If you don't promise, you won't be allowed to go outside at all. I mean it!"

They went out to the kitchen. The fudge left in the

pan and on the spoon had hardened, and Stevie set to work scraping the spoon with his teeth.

"Where's Dad and Mom?" Lynn asked as she and Mouse cut the fudge into pieces.

"They went on to the supermart from Sears. Mom said we could heat up the spaghetti sauce and she'll make the rest of the supper when they get back." She took a pan from the refrigerator and set it on the stove.

"Stevie, did Mrs. Gullone dip you in anything?" Mouse asked.

The small boy looked at her, puzzled.

"Dip me?"

"In water or milk?"

He only laughed.

Lynn tried it another way. "Did she wash your hands or face?"

This time he nodded.

"She *did*?"

"She said I was all higglety-pigglety. She talks silly sometimes. But I still like her."

Mrs. Gullone had lied about not having seen Stevie. Lynn looked fearfully toward Mouse, as Stevie took the fudge pan and spoon into the other room to watch television.

"Is . . . is that enough to . . . ?"

"For the first step, maybe," Mouse said. "Unless she's the highest power—a seventh-power witch—she can transfigure herself by dipping into water or milk, but she has to go through several different processes before she can transfigure someone else."

Judith whirled about suddenly. "Listen. Did you hear something?"

Lynn strained to hear. There was a soft, almost imperceptible bumping or thumping noise from above. "It sounds like it's coming from upstairs."

The noise came again, lighter than footsteps.

"I'm staying down here with Stevie," Mouse said shakily, her eyes huge, as Lynn and Judith headed for the hall.

"How long were you and Mouse gone?" Judith whispered. "Someone could have come in while you were away."

"Maybe fifteen minutes."

Halfway up the stairs, Lynn realized that they shouldn't be going up there by themselves. They should take Stevie, leave the house, and call the police from a neighbor's. But there was something about the sound that made her certain it was no man or woman. At the same time, that very thought—that it wasn't human—gave her goose bumps.

At the top of the stairs, they listened again. For a while all was quiet. Then the soft thud came again, from their parents' bedroom. Clinging to each other, the girls moved forward and stopped at the open door.

There was no sign of any person in the room. The bed was made. A pair of Mother's jeans lay over the arm of a chair. Dad's sneakers were on the floor under the window, his sweater on the dresser. A normal-looking bedroom.

And then, a gnawing, scratching, scraping sound.

Lynn stepped forward to see over the top of the bed, then gasped, for there at the door to the closet was the large gray rabbit, scratching to open the door that had been left standing not quite latched, but not open either.

"The rabbit!" Judith said.

The large animal turned its dark eye toward them.

"It knows where . . ." Lynn dared not finish, sure that the rabbit could understand. She did not want to say "the book" aloud, in case the rabbit only suspected where it was. But she had no doubt that the animal had come on orders from Mrs. Gullone, that it had first lured Stevie away, knowing that the girls would follow, and then backtracked and got in the house to search for *Spells and Potions*. A witch's familiar, to do her bidding.

Lynn grabbed one of her father's sneakers and started around the bed.

"Wait," said Judith. "Don't go after it yet. Let it feel comfortable with us here in the room, then we'll catch it. Just stand still."

"You know who this rabbit is, don't you?" Lynn asked her sister.

"Who?"

Lynn started to say it was Clyde Tuggle, and how she felt certain that instead of murdering her brother, as she and Mouse once suspected, Mrs. Tuggle had bodily transformed him instead. Where he had been or *what* he had been in the years before Lynn knew Mrs. Tuggle, she wasn't sure. But she felt certain that since Judith had first become involved with the old woman, they had seen Clyde Tuggle in three forms: as Mrs. Tuggle's supposed grandson, as a cat, and then a rabbit—always nearby when she needed him most.

By transfiguring a boy or girl into a familiar, a witch can keep a child his same age for a period of many years; when brought back again into his original likeness, he will be the age he was before. Lynn shivered.

She knew, however, that Judith had really liked Clyde Tuggle when he had come to visit, thinking he was Mrs. Tuggle's grandson, as he had told them.

"*Who?*" Judith asked again.

"Her familiar," Lynn answered, unsure of how Judith would feel now if she thought that the animal was Clyde. "A witch can make a servant out of an animal, and make it do anything she likes. A witch and her familiar are so close they almost become one, the book said, and she is very protective of it. I know she sent the rabbit to get you-know-what, and somehow it suspects where that is. I'm not going to wait. I want the rabbit out of here." Lynn advanced with the sneaker.

"Shoo!" she said. The rabbit pivoted and showed its teeth, like a rat. It seemed even larger than before.

"It'll go back and report to Mrs. Gullone," Judith said. "What we should do, Lynn, is capture it and keep it locked up here where it can't do any harm."

Lynn remembered all the trouble she and Mouse had had before with trapping the demon cat.

"Something would happen," Lynn said. "Believe me, Judith. It would get loose, or Stevie would open the cage, or—"

"Lynn?" came Mouse's voice hesitantly from the stairs. "What did you find?"

"The rabbit," Lynn whispered down to her, not wanting Stevie to know. "Open the front door so we can chase it out." She heard Mouse tiptoe back down, but then Stevie's voice, and his footsteps on the stairs.

"I want to capture it," Judith said stubbornly. "We could keep it in the cellar and check on it every day." She took another step forward, holding her arms out wide as if to trap the animal.

Suddenly the rabbit flew. It was the only way Lynn could describe it. It was a leap at first, but once in the air, the rabbit seemed to sail across the bed in an impossible jump, even for a rabbit. It landed once on the floor, then flew out into the hallway. Past Stevie on the stairs, past Mouse at the bottom, and through the open door.

"My rabbit!" Stevie yelled, but it was gone.

He turned accusingly to Judith and Lynn as they followed it downstairs.

"My rabbit!" he yelled. "You're mean! You don't like anything!" His face was suddenly red with anger. "You don't like Mrs. Gullone and you don't like her rabbit. You never want me to have any fun. I can go live with her! She said I could. She'll give me a new name, and I'll be *glad!*"

The girls stared in horror.

"What do you mean, Stevie, she'll give you a new name?" Lynn asked.

"She's magic! She said! She can make me any animal I want, and all I have to do is tell her, and I can even fly if I want to."

Lynn pushed the door closed and leaned against it, too frightened to respond at first. If ever she had doubted her own fears, she doubted no longer.

"I hate you!" Stevie said, a phrase he saved for his angriest moments, and plopped himself down on the stairs.

Lynn closed her eyes, waiting to catch her breath. Maybe she *was* mean, but she was capable of hating too. She felt at that moment she hated the rabbit almost more than anything else she could think of— felt she could easily kill it with her own hands. They were all capable of both good and evil thoughts, even little Stevie.

No one wanted to discuss the rabbit in front of him, however.

"Rabbits shouldn't be in the house" was all Judith told him, and then, to the others, "Let's start the spaghetti." Everyone went back to the kitchen.

As she worked at setting the table, Lynn almost told Judith about the letters of *Delcy* spelling *Clyde*. But thinking again of evil, she realized that *evil*, spelled backward, was *live*. What, exactly, did these spelling games prove? Perhaps nothing. Nothing at all.

And then she had another thought: if every person is capable of both good and evil—even Judith, even

Stevie—shouldn't there be, inside Mrs. Gullone, some deep, almost buried seed of goodness along with all that evil? It was a thought that confused her, however. She did not quite know what to make of it.

For a week things were quiet. The leaves that were turning yellow at their tips the Saturday before had yellowed completely now. The trees were ablaze with red and gold, and all up and down Lynn's street the old-fashioned gingerbread houses were surrounded by orange and rust and green.

Dr. Long was attending a convention out of town, and it had been decided that after he returned, the three men would pay a visit to Mrs. Gullone at *her* house, invite themselves in, and confront her there.

Mother, after hearing about the rabbit, had taken *Spells and Potions* from the back of her closet and put it in the top drawer of a high bureau that stood on the landing to the second-floor. The rest of the family knew where it was—all but Stevie. Lynn's little brother was the person they all tried to protect now; tried to tell him only enough to keep him from going up the street to Mrs. Gullone's, but not enough to make him fearful. But no one had any illusion that the trouble with the old woman was over, and after Lynn told her parents what Stevie had said about Mrs. Gullone's offer to turn him into any kind of animal he liked, Mother didn't let him out of her sight for a moment—even walked him to and from school.

"What's bothering me," Mouse confided to Lynn

over lunch one day at school, "is Halloween. It's another witches' Sabbat, you know. A witch's power is supposed to be greatest on a Sabbat."

What Mrs. Gullone might try on Halloween, or whether she would try anything at all, was the chief subject of conversation in the evenings after Stevie had gone to bed.

"Just be aware," Lynn's father said. "If you see or hear anything unusual, let me know. Mr. Beasley and I are both going to be patrolling the streets, and he's going to station himself up by Mrs. Gullone's the whole evening to make sure that she doesn't invite trick-or-treaters inside."

Father took Stevie out in his skeleton costume and let him go door-to-door—only *down* the hill, however, a long way from the old woman's house. Mother drove Judith to a Halloween dance at school, and stayed to help out with refreshments. Mouse came over to stay with Lynn, and together they answered the doorbell when it rang, and passed out miniature Mars bars and Tootsie Rolls.

When Betty, Charlotte Ann, and Kirsten came by, all dressed as clowns, Lynn and Mouse invited them in for a Coke before they went on again. There were little boys dressed in Spiderman costumes, older boys dressed as bandits, two girls wearing a donkey costume, and the usual assortment of ballerinas, zombies, witches, and cowboys.

At one point a large group came up the steps, laughing and making a lot of noise. Some of the boys were setting off firecrackers, and the only way Lynn and Mouse could keep them from doing mischief was to go to the edge of the porch and throw Mars bars out onto the lawn, where the children scrambled to pick them up.

As the group set off again toward the next house, Mouse said suddenly: "Someone's missing."

"What do you mean?"

"Think." Mouse looked worried. "There were two cowboys, a ghost, a zombie, a witch, and a gypsy. Right?"

"I think so. And a couple Frankensteins."

"Right. Well, look. There go the cowboys, the ghost, the Frankensteins, the zombie, and the witch, but the old gypsy is missing."

"The *old* gypsy?"

"Didn't you notice? She was all wrinkled and bent, and had a shawl around her head. . . ."

"Mrs. Gullone!" they both said together. In trying to get rid of the boys with the firecrackers, Lynn and Mouse had turned their backs on the old gypsy woman, and she might have sneaked in the house. She could well have followed such a pack of noisy children, slipped in among them, and even they might not have noticed.

The book! Lynn whirled around and raced up to the tall bureau on the landing. *Spells and Potions* was still there. If Mrs. Gullone had come for it, however, that meant she was still in the house.

"Listen," Lynn told Mouse from the top of the stairs. "I'm going to go from room to room till I find her. You stay right down here in the hall where you can see the front and back doors."

"Oh, L-Lordy, L-Lynn!" Mouse gasped.

Lynn started at the bedroom at the top of the house that she shared with Judith. Under both beds, inside both closets, under her desk—every nook and cranny.

She went down to the second floor and did the same. Even opened Stevie's toy chest, the bathroom hamper, checked the back of her parents' closet, under their bed.

When she came down to the first floor, she found that Father had come home with Stevie.

"Dad," she said, as her little brother dumped his Halloween treasures out on the dining room table, "we've got to tell you something."

Father followed them out to the kitchen, and Lynn and Mouse told him about the old gypsy.

"Have you checked the cellar?" Father asked.

"Not yet."

Mr. Morley took a flashlight and, while Lynn watched from the top of the stairs, looked in every corner, moving boxes, checking behind the furnace and water heater. Under his workbench, even.

"Empty," he said. "If she came in, she's gone. It probably *was* a child, Lynn, wearing a mask, and you just didn't see her as she ran off with the others."

Mouse and Lynn gave sighs of relief.

"What's happening up at Mrs. Gullone's?" Lynn asked.

"I saw Ed Beasley out on the street," her father said. "He says there's been no activity at her house at all. The porch light was on, and a few children

went up there and rang the bell, but no one answered."

"Good," said Mouse.

Mr. Beasley drove by for Marjorie at nine, Mother
and Judith came home from the party about eleven,
and shortly after that, everyone went to bed. Lynn,
however, decided that she would stay awake until
after midnight when Halloween was officially over.
She lay with her eyes half closed, listening to the
wind whistling through the cracks around her window. Forty-five minutes to go. She did not know
why she felt so uneasy.

The house was quiet except for the occasional
thump of furnace pipes, expanding and contracting,
the soft tick of the clock on Judith's side of the room.
It did not help that Mrs. Tuggle's old song came to
mind, word for word:

> *From the shadows of the pool,*
> *Black as midnight, thick as gruel,*
> *Come, my nymphs, and you shall be*
> *Silent images of me.*

Lynn opened her eyes and sat up on one elbow.
The words were not just in her head; she was sure of
it now. She was hearing them whispered from
somewhere in her room:

> *"Suck the honey from my lips,*
> *Dance upon my fingertips.*
> *When the darkness tolls the hour,*
> *I shall have you in my power."*

"D-Dad!" Lynn called weakly, not nearly loud enough. Like in a dream when you're chased, but cannot run.

Someone was in the room, yet Lynn could see nothing except the outline of her dresser and chair:

"Fast upon us, spirits all,
Listen for our whispered call.
Whistling kettle, tinkling bell,
Weave your web and spin your spell."

Before Lynn could open her mouth to call again, she realized that what she had mistaken for her chair in the gloom of the room was an old bent woman, now moving swiftly forward, and suddenly the woman's breath, as cold as snow, was on her face, freezing her lips into silence, and a voice rasped, "Do . . . rol . . . la! Fetch the book. Tell me where I can find it, my pretty!"

Lynn struggled to speak. "No!" she managed to whisper. "I won't!"

The breath grew colder still, until Lynn's whole face felt frozen, and the voice went on:

"Let my vision be your eyes;
Let my cunning make you wise.
Ear and nose and arm and knee,
Come, my pet; I conjure thee."

There was a stirring within Lynn, a feeling in her chest, her throat—a bad taste—a mix of memories of all the things she had ever done that had hurt someone's feelings—words said in anger, deeds done in spite. All of this now combined into a single force inside her that impelled her legs to move, her body to turn, her feet to follow.

But even as she rose up in bed, she knew that there was one thing unaffected by Mrs. Gullone's command—one thing that remained free, that could not be taken prisoner, and that was her will.

"Judith!" Lynn bellowed, even as her feet touched the floor, ready to follow. "Dad!" she screamed, with all her strength, her power.

"Lynn?" came Judith's sleepy voice from behind the curtain.

There were footsteps downstairs.

"Dorolla, *come!*" the gypsy commanded angrily, but just as Lynn started to stand up, the footsteps from below reached the stairs. Suddenly the shadowy figure of the old gypsy fled across the room, colliding with Judith, who was groping her way toward the light switch. Lynn saw the silhouette of the old woman there in the window at the far end, and then it was gone.

She stood shakily in the center of her floor when Father stumbled into the room and turned on the light.

"Lynn! What's the matter? Are you okay?"

Lynn burst into tears. "She was here, Dad! Mrs. Gullone was here! Her breath was like . . . like ice on my face, and she was trying to make me . . ." She gingerly touched her cheeks, her lips. " . . . give her the book. She tried to make me go with her."

Mother was in the room now, her robe thrown hastily over her shoulders.

"Where is she? Where did she go?"

"Out the window," Judith said. "She ran right into me, and then I saw her jump."

"Impossible!" Dad said, but the screens were off the windows now, the window itself wide-open, and when they looked, they saw the roof of the porch below, and realized it was not impossible at all.

Mother, Judith, and Lynn huddled together on Lynn's bed while Father took a flashlight and went outside, checking all around—the bushes, the garden, the shed. When he came back up, he said, "The closet door beneath the stairs was open. That's all I could find."

And then Lynn knew that it was the one place she hadn't looked. While she and Mouse were busy chasing off the boys with the firecrackers, the old gypsy had slipped in behind them and hidden in the storage closet beneath the stairs in the hallway.

Mother went pale. "You mean Mrs. Gullone was in there all evening? Just waiting?"

"Evidently."

"Did she hurt you, darling?" Mother asked Lynn.

"No. She didn't touch me. Only her breath."

"She still doesn't know where the book is, Mom, or she would have taken it," Judith said.

Lynn and Mother went down to the landing to check the high bureau drawer. *Spells and Potions* was still there. They checked Stevie's room. Stevie was asleep.

"But she'll come again, I'm sure of it," Mother said. "Richard, what are we going to do? Can't we file charges?"

"We can, but for what? Breaking and entering? No doors were forced. Assault? She didn't even touch Lynn. And who's going to believe that an elderly woman could have jumped out of a third-floor window, even onto a porch roof?"

Lynn, remembering the woman's strength and speed, said, "Mrs. Gullone could; I'm sure of it."

"It's time to get rid of the book," said Father. "I suggest our safe-deposit box at the bank."

"But if she still *thinks* it's here, Richard. . . . And even if she knows it's in a safe-deposit box, she'll use the children to try to get the key. You know she will."

"If only we could have trapped her here in the room," said Judith.

Mr. Morley shook his head. "I doubt even that would hold up in court. She could say she was confused. Got in the wrong house. The fact that she called you by some other name, Lynn, would only convince a judge that she thought she was in some other house. It's not only witchcraft we're dealing with here, but a very cunning woman."

Mrs. Morley hugged Lynn. "Oh, sweetheart. What she might have done!"

Lynn hugged back. "You know what? I'm stronger than I thought. But I'm still really worried for Stevie."

"I'm going over there in the morning," Father said. "I'll confront her myself."

And the next day he did. He knocked repeatedly on Mrs. Gullone's door, he reported, but no one came. He went back again in the evening. No one answered. He tried the next day and the next. The house was strangely quiet.

chapter thirteen

What happened next was that Judith got a letter from Clyde Tuggle. At least, the signature said "Clyde," but it was written in Mrs. Tuggle's handwriting. Mother had an old rent receipt from the time she had used one of Mrs. Tuggle's rooms as a writing studio, and a comparison of the g's and t's showed it had obviously been written by the same person.

Dear Judith, the letter read. *I hope you still remember me. After my grandmother died in the fire, I didn't feel like writing anyone at all for a while. But now I would like to come again, at least to visit the place where she once lived. My great-aunt Greta has invited me to stay a few weeks with her. Could I see you again? Just let Mrs. G. know. I hope the answer is yes. Clyde.*

Judith stared at the letter in her hand. "What am I going to *do*, Mother?"

"Nothing," said Mother firmly. "We are going to do nothing. No answer. No response at all to Mrs. Gullone."

"It seems so impolite . . ."

This is exactly what Lynn had feared. That somehow, deep down, Judith would not be able to accept that the boy she had once liked could possibly be anyone who could harm her.

"It's obvious to me what Mrs. Gullone is up to next," Dr. Long said when the family called him over. "Somehow the boy is going to try to persuade Judith to give the book to him. Judith, believe me, this is something you just can't get involved with. It's far too dangerous."

Reluctantly, Judith agreed. No letter was sent, no phone call made.

"Mother," Lynn said when Judith was out of the room. "I want to tell you something, and I know it sounds weird."

"Nothing could possibly be more weird than what has been happening lately," said Mother.

"This could be all coincidence and not prove anything: I haven't even told Dad because he'd say it wouldn't hold up in court. But the exact same letters that spell Greta Gullone spell Elnora Tuggle, and the same letters that spell Delcy spell Clyde."

Mother frowned a little and scribbled the names on a piece of paper, working it out for herself.

"I don't know what to say, Lynn," she said at last. "I don't even know what to think."

"Me either," Lynn told her.

Mr. Morley, Mr. Beasley, and Dr. Long, all three, went to Mrs. Gullone's house on three successive evenings. They knocked repeatedly. Again the old woman never came.

But for Lynn, things always seemed just one step away from disaster. If there were no answer from

Judith, would Mrs. Gullone let Clyde remain a rabbit, or would she still transform him back into the
boy he once was? If he came by to see Judith, even
uninvited, how could she refuse to talk to him at the
door? And if she talked to him at the door, wouldn't
she feel obliged to invite him in? And once inside, he
could search out the house, bit by bit, and eventually find where the book was hidden.

No one, however, expected what happened next,
least of all Mr. Morley. It was a Tuesday night,
Stevie was in bed, Judith was doing homework at
the dining room table, Mother was sewing a quilt,
and Lynn was finishing up the dinner dishes. Father
was due home late from a meeting, and as Lynn put
the plates from the dishwasher into the cupboard,
she thought she heard his car turning into the driveway.

He did not come in right away, however, and by
the time she got to the silverware, she went to the
window to peer out into the darkness. She was just
walking into the living room to ask if Dad had come
in, when the front door opened and Mr. Morley appeared, looking somewhat upset.

"Darnedest thing happened," he said, taking off
his jacket and dropping it over the arm of the sofa.
"I'm afraid I ran over the gray rabbit."

Mother looked up. Lynn stared.

"I didn't mean to! I pulled into the driveway, and
there it was—stunned by my headlights, I guess. I
put on my brakes, of course, and it finally hopped
over to one side, so I moved forward again. Suddenly it changed direction and ran right in front of

me. It must have felt trapped over by the trashcans and panicked. I felt the thump as I hit it."

Mother put one hand to her face. "Is it dead?"

"No. But I injured one of its back legs. I got out to see if I could catch it and take it to the vet, but it got away from me. The last I saw, it was limping off toward the back of the house. I searched the yard and garden, but couldn't find it."

"Mrs. Gullone calls it her pet," Lynn said. "She told Stevie she named it Delcy."

Father leaned against the bookcase. "Well, I couldn't help it. I'll stop by Mrs. Gullone's tomorrow and tell her what happened. That is, if she'll answer the door. If it returns to her house, I'll offer to take it to the animal clinic."

"She'll be furious," Lynn said softly.

Judith came in from the dining room and sat down on the edge of the couch. "Why?"

"Because I don't think it's just a rabbit, Judith. I think it's somebody she's transformed."

"Lynn," her father said wearily. "Are we talking facts here or speculation?"

Lynn shrugged. "It's nothing I can prove. We've got worries enough for one evening, I guess."

The next afternoon, when her father drove in after work, Lynn was watching and went out to the car. "What did she say?"

"Who?"

"Mrs. Gullone. When you told her about the rabbit."

"I forgot to go by. I'll drive up now."

Without waiting to be asked, Lynn opened the door and slid in the seat beside him. She wondered what this would do to Mrs. Gullone's plan to bring Clyde Tuggle back into the picture, to have him become Judith's boyfriend again, and somehow get the book from her. If there were a boy living at Mrs. Gullone's, Lynn thought, she might notice signs that her father would miss, and that's why she wanted to go.

Mrs. Gullone's house was dark except for a light just inside the front door.

"This is the way it's been," said her father. "The one light burning just inside. But she won't answer. Maybe if she sees you, she will."

The front yard was eerie-looking now. The small saplings Mrs. Gullone had uprooted and turned upside down took up most of the space. The roots, protruding outward in all directions, gave her yard the appearance of a maze, a web, a trap, and Lynn could well imagine that if any children wandered into her yard and tried to get out again, Mrs. Gullone would have time to come out and catch them before they found their way to the street again.

They pushed past the branches of the thorn apple tree, weaved in and out of the dirt-covered roots of the saplings that overhung the narrow walk, and finally went together up the steps. Lynn waited while her father grasped the brass door-knocker and rapped a few times.

For a while it seemed as though no one would come. The breeze rustled the branches of the thorn apple, shook the dry roots of the saplings so that they made a crackling sound. And then Lynn heard a distinct whisper:

> *"Sing of morning, sing of noon,*
> *Sing of evening's silver moon"* . . .

She glanced over at her father. He was looking uncertainly about him.

"Do you hear that, Dad?"

He nodded.

> *"Feel the darkness, touch the black,*
> *Hear the shadows whisper back."*

Then, whether by a slight sound from indoors or a movement behind the empty eyes of the troll, Lynn sensed someone behind the door, and finally the handle turned, the door opened, and the small, withered woman peered out at them, her eyes sharp and dark.

"Eh? The Morleys?" She was holding a stick or a cane, Lynn couldn't tell which, and seemed to lean on it as she studied them intently. "Have you come about my rabbit?"

That's what would bring her to the door, Lynn decided. News of her rabbit.

"Yes, I have, Mrs. Gullone. I came to tell you that I had a small accident with my car," Lynn's father said, getting right to the point. "Last night, as I was pulling in my driveway, your rabbit ran in front of me, and I struck one of its hind legs."

There was no mistaking the anger in the woman's eyes. " 'Twas *you*, then."

"I beg your pardon?"

"Who hurt my Delcy."

"Then the rabbit came back? I'll be glad to take it to a veterinarian and—"

Suddenly the stick slipped out of Mrs. Gullone's hand and rolled away from her—and as the old woman moved to retrieve it, Lynn stared, speechless, for Mrs. Gullone was limping badly. *The witch and her familiar are as one.*

"I tried to catch it, to take it to the animal clinic and have its leg reset, but it hopped away," Father went on.

"It has not come back to me, Mr. Morley."

"Well, I'm very sorry, then." Father looked confused. "But I thought . . . well, if you'll let me know if it does, I'll be glad to . . ."

"You'll have no one look at my rabbit. It's trouble enough you've caused already."

"*Me!* If it's trouble we're talking about . . ."

"An old woman has few enough pleasures, but one of mine was to bundle up of an evening and sit out in my garden, watching the dark come in, and my gray rabbit dance about in the leaves."

"Well, it was an accident, and, as I said, I'm sorry."

"If sorry you be, you will find for me a book that has salves and potions for animals such as mine, for it is a rare animal, unlike any other. *Spells and Potions* is the name, Mr. Morley, and if you know where it is, I shall pay a pretty penny for it."

Lynn could not believe she had asked for it outright.

"You seem to have great faith in a book, Mrs. Gullone, and are willing to pay a large amount for it, when I could have your rabbit healed without any cost at all to you."

"I want the book."

"It's not for sale," Father said. "Furthermore, you were in our house the other night and accosted our daughter."

"You speak nonsense, my man."

"You were in my daughter's bedroom. Both Lynn and Judith saw you jump from the window."

"You are raving! This poor old woman can scarcely make it down the steps, much less jump from a window."

"All I'm saying, Mrs. Gullone, is that if I find you in our house again, I will file charges. Is that clearly understood?" And when she did not answer, he said, "Let's go, Lynn," and turned away.

But Lynn's feet seemed glued to the spot, and her eyes to the eyes of the old woman in front of her, one of them gray and one green, never blinking.

"We shall see," Lynn heard her murmur. "We shall see, my fine man, what will be."

There were no more letters from Clyde Tuggle. Each day after school, Lynn and Mouse, carrying a cage from the Humane Society, went looking for the gray rabbit—all across the field behind the garden and along Cowden's Creek—but there was no sign of it.

"It's all true, Lynn," Mouse breathed. "She's hurt the same as her familiar."

"I know. I asked Dad which of the rabbit's legs he had struck, and he said the left hind leg. It's Mrs. Gullone's left leg that limps. But he thinks it was her jump from the window that hurt her."

"My dad said he saw Mrs. Gullone in town with her market basket, and she was limping badly. She had to sit down on the steps of the courthouse to rest," Mouse said.

Lynn told her mother, but not quite all. She didn't have to. Mrs. Morley had been reading *Spells and Potions* and had already guessed.

"You think that Delcy is her familiar, don't you, Lynn?"

"Yes."

"But regardless of what caused her condition," Mother went on, "that woman needs to see a doctor. Judith," she called as Judith came in from school, "I want you and Lynn to come along with me. We're going to see if the three of us can persuade Mrs. Gullone to let us take her to a doctor."

"After all she's *done*, Mother?"

"Yes. Because I think if we could get a doctor on the case, someone else would begin to see her for what she really is. We wouldn't be the only ones suspecting witchcraft."

"Where's Stevie?"

"At a birthday party."

It felt strange to be walking up the hill—the three of them—to a place they knew they should not go, but on a mission they could not help.

"Lynn," Judith said, "does that rabbit's injury have anything to do with Mrs. Gullone's leg?"

"We think so," Lynn said, and explained about a witch and her familiar. But she said nothing about bodily transfiguration, and nothing at all about Clyde Tuggle.

Lynn did not know how it was possible, but the roots of the dead saplings, standing upside down in Mrs. Gullone's yard, seemed to have grown, as though nurtured by something other than rain and soil. They twisted and intertwined like the rope in a fisherman's net, and it took some doing to get past the waist-high roots and then the branches of the thorn apple tree to reach the door.

Again there was the long wait after Mother had used the door knocker, and again Lynn sensed a presence behind the heavy door as the eyes of the troll seemed to move. And when the door opened at last, Lynn saw that the old woman was even more bent than she'd been before.

"You've come with the book?" she asked when she saw them. "Or have you found my rabbit?"

"Neither one, Mrs. Gullone," Mother said. "You really ought to see a doctor about your leg. Please let us take you in a taxi. I've called our physician, and he could see you anytime at all this afternoon."

"I've cured myself many a time before, and I'll do it again," said the old woman. "Had I my book of cures, I would have been fit by now."

"*Your* book, Mrs. Gullone?"

"Aye. The book for those who know how to use it."

"*Won't* you come with us?" Mother pleaded.

"There's naught can cure me but the book," Mrs. Gullone said stubbornly.

And so they turned away.

It was not only Lynn who heard the whispers now. Mouse said that she and her father had heard the singing while they had their supper: "Suck the honey from my lips, dance upon my fingertips." . . .

Mr. Morley had heard the whispers again when he was shaving: "When the darkness tolls the hour, I shall have you in my power."

Dr. Long did not hear them himself, but he considered it very unlikely that the Morleys and Beasleys would have heard whispers, chants, and singing merely by imagination.

Lynn and Judith heard them almost nightly. Sometimes the singing seemed to come through the open window. Other times it seemed as close to Lynn as her head, and she would rise up on one elbow, pawing at the darkness, moving her hand back and forth to see if anyone was there. Nothing there but the whisper: "Whistling kettle, tinkling bell, weave your web and spin your spell."

"I wanted to write Mom all about this," Mouse told Lynn as they walked back from the bus stop one day after school. "It would have been something big to talk about, you know? I figured maybe she'd be worried enough to call. . . ." She paused.

"Or come back?" Lynn asked gently.

"Yeah. I guess that was it. Dad said that since Mom wouldn't be coming home again no matter what, it would only worry her because there was nothing she could do."

"He's right, isn't he?"

"I guess so."

Lynn's own mother seemed to be trying to keep the household going as normally as possible—each day, each evening, the same as the one before. As always, Lynn found her working on her manuscript when she got home from school.

Once, when she took a break, Lynn asked her, "Can you talk about your book yet? Are you close enough to being finished?"

"It's based on something my own grandmother told me about a plague of grasshoppers coming when she was a little girl—so many grasshoppers that they got in your hair and clothes if you stepped outside."

Lynn remembered her mother telling her that story once. But she also remembered how Mother's books sometimes resembled real life, an almost eerie forecast of things to come. She was thinking about the night she set fire to the witch weed, and how, even before she struck the match, the crickets and grasshoppers seemed to know what she was about, because they began fleeing in huge swarms— armies of crickets and grasshoppers.

"What happened?" Lynn asked.

"Well, I'm not sure how my book is going to end yet, but what happened to Grandmother is that the family was very hungry that year. The grass- hoppers destroyed their crops, the cow died, and my grandmother had a new baby kitten that almost starved to death. It was only her faithful care that pulled it through."

"Did the grasshoppers ever come back?"

"Not while she was on the farm. She said that once she had lived through that, she felt she could live through anything."

Maybe that was how she would feel when, and if, this whole witchcraft business was over, Lynn thought; that if she survived this, she could live through anything. She got out *Spells and Potions* one evening and read through the pages carefully, looking for cures for a familiar, thinking that she might write them down and have Mother give them to Mrs. Gullone, if she did. She found several, all right, but each involved harm to someone else, and when Lynn showed them to Mother, it was agreed that the book should remain where it was. Under no circumstances should Mrs. Gullone have it.

It was waiting that was the hardest. Lynn wondered if she only imagined it, but every day seemed quieter than the one before. Unnaturally quiet. Not a cheep nor chirp. No rain, no wind. As though the whole neighborhood were holding its breath.

chapter fourteen

On Monday evening, Dr. Long, Mouse, and her father came to the Morleys' for another meeting. It was good to have Mother in on it this time.

"We have a problem of a different sort," Father said, explaining about the rabbit. "The whispers and chants have grown stronger—we've all heard them now—but Mrs. Gullone herself seems to be ill."

Mr. Beasley nodded. "One of my customers told me he was driving by her house yesterday, and saw her trying to get down her walk to pick up the newspaper. Her clothes caught on the roots and branches that are growing out of control all over her front lawn, and she fell. He stopped and helped her get to her feet, but she insisted she didn't need a doctor."

Lynn and Mouse looked at each other.

"It's because of the rabbit," Lynn said aloud.

Everyone turned to look at her.

"I . . . *we* believe . . . Mouse and I . . . that the rabbit is her 'familiar'—and whatever happens to the familiar happens to the witch. If the rabbit is wounded, then Mrs. Gullone is wounded too, and will stay just as sick as the rabbit."

There was silence for a moment.

"Richard," Mother said, "I don't care if that woman *is* a witch, or what caused her injury, we ought to get her to the hospital. Then she would be under medical supervision, and if her wounds are supernatural, it's up to the doctors to check further. We've got to do it."

"Do you want us to carry her there bodily?" Lynn's father said. "You know she doesn't want to go, Sylvia."

The group sat silently about the living room, each wondering what to do next.

"This is the strangest case I've come across," Dr. Long said at last. "Every time I consider bringing it up at a psychology conference, I realize how ridiculous it would sound. Mrs. Morley is right, however; if we *could* get her to a hospital, the medical profession would be obliged to study her case. When doctors, who know nothing about her, observe some of the things we've seen—then perhaps what we have to tell them won't seem so incredible."

"And if her injury *is* connected to the rabbit, then I feel personally responsible to get help for her," Father said.

"Does *any*one else have anything to offer— anything at all that would help?" Mr. Beasley looked around the circle. "We need all the suggestions we can get."

"Marjorie, we haven't heard from you this evening," Dr. Long said.

"I wish ..." Mouse said softly, "that if witchcraft is strong enough to do some of the things we think it's done, it could..." She took a deep breath.

"Well," she said, "it can't." And everyone knew what she meant.

"I know," said her father. "And you're right, honey. It can't."

"There's one more thing, though," Lynn put in. "When I was looking for cures for the rabbit, I found something on the very last page of the book that I hadn't noticed before, but I don't understand it."

"Could I see it?" asked Dr. Long.

Lynn went upstairs, past the room where Stevie was sleeping, and got *Spells and Potions* from the top drawer of the high dresser in the hallway. Downstairs again, she sat on the couch between Mouse and Judith and read aloud:

"Strong as a witch's spell, great as a warlock's curse, swift as the wing of a crow, the scratch of a cat, or the leap of a hare, there is something more powerful still that witches fear; it can overcome the deadliest potion, tame the wildest demon, annul all threats, turn cruel into kind, and thus put an end to witchcraft. The truth is this . . ." Lynn stopped reading. "The rest is in a foreign language or something." She gave the book to Dr. Long.

The psychologist studied the last yellowed page of *Spells and Potions*, its edges curled, small flakes of paper breaking off into his hand. "It's in Latin," he said. "I'm afraid that's not one of my specialties."

"Perhaps I can read it," said Marjorie's father, and the book was passed to him.

The big man with the bushy mustache put on his reading glasses and ran one finger along the words in the last line. "Vincite malum bono," he said thoughtfully. And then, to the others: "Overcome evil with good."

There was no sound at all in the living room for a time.

"It's something we knew all along, isn't it?" Mother said at last.

"Well, it's what we're *trying* to do," said Judith. "Maybe if we *all* went up to see her, we could convince her to go to a hospital."

"A neighborhood delegation, so to speak," said Dr. Long. "Judith's right. I think it would help if you girls went too. Young people can often persuade when older folks can't."

Mother stood up. "Let's try it. Let's just go up the hill right now, and gently surround her, coax her into getting in the car."

"I'll drive on up, and meet the rest of you out in front," said Dr. Long, getting out his car keys. "If she agrees to go, some of you had better ride in the car with us."

Lynn got her jacket.

"I don't want to leave Stevie here by himself," Mother said. "Lynn, wake him gently, would you, and tell him we're going for a walk. Mrs. Gullone likes him. Maybe if he was along, she'd change her mind."

Lynn went up to Stevie's room and leaned over him. "Stevie," she said softly. "Are you asleep?"

He made little blowing noises from his lips, but his eyelids fluttered. Her heart beat faster. Despite Mrs. Gullone's frailty, her whispers and chants were getting stronger. Was it possible that going up there could be one huge mistake? That by taking little Stevie, they were exposing him to danger?

"Stevie," she said again, having no choice. "We're all going for a walk up the hill in the dark."

Now the eyes opened. "I just got to bed!" he protested groggily.

"I know, but Mother doesn't want you here alone, and we're all going to go." And then, remembering the last line of the book, she said, "We need you to help us. Mrs. Gullone is sick, and we want to take her to a doctor to make her well."

Stevie sleepily crawled out of bed and Lynn helped him put on his slippers and jacket.

"I thought you didn't like Mrs. Gullone," he yawned, teetering back and forth as Lynn zipped his jacket.

"I don't like what she does sometimes, but I want to see her get well, and you can help us. We need you along to think good things about her, Stevie. Listen. When we go up there, I want you to think about the nicest things she's ever said or done for you, okay? Just fill your head with good thoughts."

Stevie squinted at her in confusion, but followed her down the stairs where the others were putting on their coats, and the small procession started out the door—Mother, Father, and Mr. Beasley walking in front, Judith and Stevie next, Mouse and Lynn at the back of the line.

"I feel weird, Lynn," Mouse confided.

"Me too. Like it's the end of something."

"Of us, probably," said Mouse. "When she sees us

coming, she'll pull out all the stops. She'll try every spell, every trick she knows."

"Maybe."

The moon was full. The others had gotten farther ahead, and were walking along the sidewalk by the empty lot now, while Lynn and Mouse had just reached the hedge. All of a sudden Mouse grabbed Lynn's arm, and Lynn looked where she was pointing. The large gray rabbit, its body bony and thin, was moving slowly along the hedge, one leg dragging behind it. When it saw the girls, it made a sound that Lynn had never heard before—something between a moan and a growl.

"Oh, Lordy!" Mouse gasped. "She'll hate us, Lynn. She'll kill us all! I don't think we should do this. I don't think we should go up there."

Lynn moved up on the grass, thinking that she might be able to grab the rabbit, but despite its injured leg, it disappeared into the darkness. Lynn went on shakily beside Mouse. For a moment or two, she felt like calling to the others and telling them not to go. Felt like turning back to the safety of her own room. But, at the same time, she knew there was no safety at all, not even in her own home, her own family, her own room, as long as Mrs. Gullone, or Mrs. Tuggle, could control them. And with each step forward, she felt her strength return.

"Mouse, think about it," she said. "*Overcome evil with good*. Do you remember how, when we were trapped in Mrs. Tuggle's basement, we drew that

circle around us to keep her out? What if this time
we made a circle around her to keep the evil in?"

"Lynn, that's too scary."

"Not any scarier than thinking what all she could
do if she ever got her hands on *Spells and Potions.*"

Dr. Long was waiting for them at the curb outside
Mrs. Gullone's house. There were no lights on in the
house at all. Lynn remembered how Mrs. Tuggle
used to sit around in the evening in darkness, sometimes only a candle lighting the room.

It was difficult to get up the sidewalk because the
roots of the strange saplings almost blocked the way
entirely. The thorn apple tree spread out its
branches as though to keep anyone from entering,
and when they reached the porch at last and Lynn's
father rapped, there was no noise from inside—no
answer, no footsteps, no movement behind the eyes
of the troll.

And then the whispers came:

> *"Sing of morning, sing of noon,*
> *Sing of evening's silver moon.*
> *Touch the darkness, feel the black,*
> *Hear the shadows whisper back."*

"She said that sometimes she sits in the backyard at night," Lynn said. "She used to sit out
there with her rabbit." She did not mention that
the rabbit looked half dead, that they had seen it
on the way.

"Maybe the rabbit came back!" Stevie said hopefully, more awake now, as they moved quietly around the house.

Lynn was suddenly conscious of sound again. Even though it was November, even though it was dark, crows screeched back and forth somewhere in the trees above. As though everything were coming alive now. Everything seemed to be watching. Waiting.

The backyard was misty, but Lynn could just make out the figure of an old woman, sitting in a chair in her garden, which was dry now, the flowers dead. A shawl was wrapped around her head and shoulders, and her hands were thrust up the arms of her dress for warmth. Her head turned when she heard them coming.

"Hello, Mrs. Gullone," Dr. Long called out, so as not to startle her. "We were all out for a walk, and thought we'd come by to see how you are doing."

"You have come to steal my power," said Mrs. Gullone accusingly.

"We've come only to get help for your leg if we can," Father told her. "You really can't go on like this, you know—scarcely able to get about."

"Stay away from me," the old woman warned, her voice strident, and Lynn noticed a strange and sudden wind arise from out of the ground, from the grasses around the old woman's feet.

"Greta, we can't let you stay here alone," Mrs. Morley repeated as the group enclosed her. "We know that your leg is worse, that you're having trouble walking. You've fallen, even. The whole neighborhood is worried about you."

Mrs. Gullone jerked her head first one way, then another, shrinking away from the group. "Where did you learn this? Keep away, I tell you!"

And Lynn knew that her hunch was right. She knew that as surely as the consecrated chalk circle, drawn around her and Mouse in Mrs. Tuggle's cellar, had once kept evil out, a circle of goodwill might work the other way and trap Mrs. Gullone's evilness inside it—squeeze it to nothing.

"Hold hands," she said to Mouse on one side of her, Judith on the other. The girls stretched out their hands, and the grown-ups, uncertain, took hold, Stevie between Mom and Dad.

Mrs. Gullone gave a shrill cry and tried to stand up. "No!" she shrieked. "Dorolla! Sevena!"

The wind grew stronger yet, but Lynn felt stronger than the wind even. She planted her feet firmly on the ground and let the gale blow about her, whipping her jacket, tossing her hair.

If Mrs. Gullone could summon the potential for evil inside of others, then perhaps Lynn could summon up something from long ago in Mrs. Gullone—something that had once been good and innocent, before the witchcraft began. She remembered what Mother had found out from a woman on the Isle of Man, that when Elnora was a little girl, they called her Ellie. Ellie Martin. And, sure that Greta Gullone was the same Mrs. Tuggle who had lived here before, Lynn called out, as the little circle moved closer, "Ellie? Ellie Martin?"

Instantly a black cloud covered the moon, darkening the whole backyard. The wind blew and whis-

tled in their ears, and Lynn bent her head against the onslaught. But still the circle remained, still their hands held fast. The moon came out again.

"Say her name," Lynn pleaded with the others. "The name she had—we know she had—as a little girl."

"Ellie!" the others called. "Ellie Martin."

There was a shriek from the crumpled figure there in the chair, then another, higher in pitch, and still another, softer now, that sounded like a baby crying.

More darkness rolled through the backyard like a thundercloud coming from the west, bringing in fog, and when it had passed, the group looked where the old woman had been sitting. There was only a heap of clothing on the chair.

No one spoke, not even Stevie, who had whimpered only once when the wind was strongest. Lynn was almost afraid to look around the circle, for fear she would find someone missing, someone changed.

At last Father moved forward and lifted the shawl, and there beneath it, on the chair, was the cold, stiff body of the gray rabbit.

Stevie began to cry. Mother picked him up and held him, and the others stared mutely at each other, knowing that what had happened here was nothing they could ever explain.

"It's truly unbelievable, isn't it?" murmured Dr. Long.

But suddenly, from beneath the chair, came a tiny cry, so soft that Lynn might have missed it had she not been listening for one last song, one last whisper. Mouse heard it too.

"Listen!" Mouse said.

They all paused, and Stevie stopped crying. The sound came again. Mouse crept forward and gingerly lifted the clothing that hung down from the seat of the chair, and there on the grass was a tiny kitten—a calico kitten of white, red, and brown—so small, so young, that its eyes were barely open.

"Oh, Lynn!" Mouse breathed. She gently lifted it up in her hands and held it close to her chest, where it nuzzled her neck and squealed again.

"A kitty!" cried Stevie, breaking into smiles.

"Such a *new* little thing," said Mother as Stevie reached out to pet it.

Lynn watched as Marjorie put her face next to the kitten, cooing at it, grinning as it licked her cheek. Mouse looked at her father, and without waiting for her question, he answered, "Yes, you may keep it."

Was it over, then? Was it really, truly over? Lynn looked up at the house where so much had happened. The windows were dark. It looked deserted, abandoned for all time.

"I think, at last, we may go home," said Dr. Long.

The wind that had whipped through the backyard at gale force only minutes ago had become a breeze, the mist had thinned, and the feathery outline of trees and branches appeared once more in the moonlight. The only sound now was the soft exchange between Mouse and her new kitten. No chants, no songs, no whispers.

If Lynn herself were asked to describe what had

happened, she thought, she would say that as the circle closed in on Mrs. Gullone—Mrs. Tuggle—the evil had turned in upon itself, squeezed tighter and tighter. What was left was the small seed of goodness that had once, long ago, been a young girl named Ellie Martin, and wanting to live after being prisoner for so long, the goodness had sprung into life as a kitten.

"It's over," Lynn said, putting one arm around her mother, and Mother hugged back.

"I'm sure of it," said her father.

To Mouse, Lynn asked, "What are you going to name the kitten?"

"M.L. Short for Mouse-Lynn. Little Mouselynn. That's who it is."

"That kitten needs some milk," Mother told her. "I'll warm some on the stove. I think I've got a medicine dropper we can use to feed it. Why don't you all stop by our house and I'll put some coffee on for the rest of us, cocoa for the children."

They started down the hill again, the kitten under Marjorie's chin, Stevie skipping happily alongside in his slippers, reaching up now and then to pet it. The calico kitten was nuzzling Marjorie's face, and Mouse made happy little squeaks herself, smiling more broadly than Lynn had seen her do for months and months.

It was over at last—really, truly over—and with little Mouselynn, for whom everything was fresh and new, this was a wonderful beginning.

PHYLLIS REYNOLDS NAYLOR now concludes the sequel trilogy to her first three witch books. Raised on Grimms' fairy tales, she decided to write six novels of the supernatural: *Witch's Sister, Witch Water, The Witch Herself, The Witch's Eye, Witch Weed,* and *The Witch Returns,* which are an eerie combination of fantasy and realism.

Mrs. Naylor has written over seventy books. Her book *Shiloh* was awarded the Newbery Medal. Her work has received other numerous awards, including the Edgar Allan Poe Award, the Christopher Award, the Child Study Award, and the Annual Book Award from the Society of School Librarians International.

JOE BURLESON attended Art Center College of Design in Pasadena and lives in Portland, Oregon.